Go ahead and scream.

No one can hear you. You're no longer in the safe world you know.

You've taken a terrifying step . . .

into the darkest corners of your imagination.

You've opened the door to . . .

the
NiGHTMARE
rOOm

the NIGHTMARE room

Don't Forget Me!

R.L. STINE

AVON BOOKS

An Imprint of HarperCollinsPublishers

PARACHUTE PRESS

Don't Forget Me!

Printed in the United States of America.

For information address:
HarperCollins Children's Books,
a division of HarperCollins Publishers,
1350 Avenue of the Americas,
New York, NY 10019.

Library of Congress Catalog Card Number: 00-101108
ISBN 0-06-440899-X

First Avon edition, 2000

AVON TRADEMARK REG. US. PAT. OFF. AND IN OTHER
COUNTRIES, MARCA REGISTRADA, HECHO EN USA

Visit us on the World Wide Web!
www.harperchildrens.com

Welcome...

For all of us there's a place where true horror waits—our own personal Nightmare Room. You might find it anywhere—at home, at school, in the woods, at the mall . . . in your MIND. Take one step, shut your eyes—and you're there. You've crossed the line. You've crossed over, from reality to nightmare.

I'm R.L. Stine. Let me introduce you to Danielle Warner. She's that worried-looking girl with the solemn, dark eyes.

Danielle has been very tense lately. Anyone would be tense moving into an old house with long shadows, creaking doors, mysterious groans, and whispers.

And now, Danielle's brother, Peter, is frightening her. He is acting strange—strange and dangerous. And it might be Danielle's fault.

Maybe she shouldn't have told Peter she wished she was an only child. Sure, she was only joking. But Danielle is about to learn a terrifying lesson. Sometimes your most evil wishes come true . . . in THE NIGHTMARE ROOM.

I wrapped my hands around my brother's throat and started to tighten them. "Die, monster, die!" I screamed.

Peter spun out of my grasp. "Danielle, give me a break," he groaned, rubbing his throat. "You're about as funny as head lice."

My friend Addie laughed. She thinks everything Peter says is funny.

"I know what we can do for the talent show at school," I told her. "A magic act. We can make Peter disappear."

Peter stuck his tongue out at me. It was purple from the grape soda he was drinking.

Mom appeared in the kitchen carrying a tall stack of dinner plates. She set them down on the counter next to the piles of bowls and cups she had unpacked. She blew a strand of hair off her forehead and frowned at me. "Danielle, stop saying things like that about your little brother. You'd feel terrible if anything happened to Peter."

"Yeah. Terrible," I said, rolling my eyes. "But I'd get over it in a minute or two."

"Mom, do you know what Danielle said?" Peter asked in a tiny, hurt voice. "She said her birthday wish is to be an only child!"

Mom scowled at me. "You didn't really say that to Peter, did you?"

"Of course not," I replied, glaring at Peter, who was still pretending to be hurt. "I mean, maybe I said it. But it was just a joke."

"Your face is a joke!" Peter said.

Addie laughed again.

Why does she think Peter is such a riot? Why do all my friends think he's so adorable and funny?

Mom narrowed her eyes at me. "Danielle, you're fifteen and Peter is nine. You're supposed to be the grown-up. You have to take care of him."

"No problem," I said. I raised my hands to strangle him again. "I'll be glad to take care of him!" I dove at him.

Peter laughed and squirmed away.

It was the kind of kidding around brothers and sisters do all the time. Nothing to it, really. It was all so innocent and good-natured.

I had no idea what was to come in the next few days.

I had no idea I really was about to lose my brother.

It all started that day, the day Addie came to see our new house.

Mom had picked up a stack of china saucers and was carrying it to a cabinet above the stove. "Danielle, are you going to help me unpack this stuff?" she asked. "We've only got about a hundred more cartons to open."

"I'll open some!" Peter volunteered eagerly. He chugged the rest of his grape soda and tossed the can to the counter. "I'll open all of them!"

Mom shook her head. "I don't want to open all of them now. Just the ones for the kitchen."

"Let me help!" Peter cried.

I motioned to Addie to follow me. "I'll help right after I give Addie the house tour," I told Mom.

Addie tossed her blond ponytail behind her shoulders and hopped down from the kitchen stool. "I can't wait to see your new house, Mrs. Warner," she said cheerfully.

Addie is a very cheerful girl. That's her thing. She

even wears cheerful colors. Today she had a silky pink vest over a blue T-shirt and bright orange capri pants she bought at some thrift store for two dollars.

Outrageous colors! But Addie always looked really together.

The red-and-blue glass beads she wore every day clattered as she started across the kitchen. Addie has a lot of style. I like things kind of plain and simple. My favorite color is gray. She always makes me feel brighter just walking beside me.

"Whoa." Mom stepped in front of Addie, blocking her way. "Did you get your ears pierced again?"

Addie nodded.

Mom carefully examined the white and gold hoops in Addie's ears. "Three in each ear?"

Addie nodded again. "Yeah. Only three."

Peter pushed in between Mom and Addie. "Hey, Mom, can I get my nose pierced?"

Mom's mouth dropped open but no sound came out.

I picked up the hammer Dad had been using. "Here, Peter," I said. "I'll do it for you."

Peter stuck out his purple tongue again.

"Stop picking on Peter," Mom said.

"Boohoo." Peter rubbed his eyes and pretended to cry. "She hurt my feelings."

I dropped the hammer, grabbed Addie's arm, and tugged her to the kitchen door. "Come on. The grand house tour. I'm showing off this magnificent mansion." I stepped over a pile of carpentry tools.

"Be careful," Mom called after us. "The molding in the back hall was just painted. And there are still a few floorboards missing back there."

"We'll be careful," I said.

"I want to give the tour!" Peter shouted, running after Addie and me. "We can start in my room. I have the coolest window seat. When we unpack my binoculars, I can sit there and spy on the neighbors. And my closet's bigger than my old bedroom. And I think there's a secret compartment in the wall!"

"Very cool," Addie agreed, her long ponytail swaying behind her as she walked toward the front stairs.

"Peter, why don't you help Mom," I suggested. "I'm going to show Addie around myself. Maybe we'll look at your room later."

"No way!" he cried. "Addie wants to see my room first, right?" He clamped himself around her arm and started to pull.

Addie laughed. "Well—"

"Peter?" Mom called from the kitchen. "Peter? Can you come back here? I really need your help."

Peter groaned and let go of Addie. "I'll be back," he muttered. "Don't do my room without me." He stomped away, the cuffs of his baggy jeans scraping the floor.

Addie shook her head. "Your brother is so sweet."

I rolled my eyes. "Easy for you to say. I think he's totally annoying."

She snickered. "You're both such opposites in every way. You're so quiet and serious, and Peter never stops talking. Look at him. Red hair. Bright red glasses. All those freckles and pale, white skin. He looks like an elf. And then look at you. You're so dark and adult looking. Dark brown eyes, wavy brown hair. It's like you're not from the same family."

"That's because Peter comes from Mars," I said.

Addie stopped at the stairway and gazed around at the peeling wallpaper, the cracked plaster, the long, uncarpeted halls. "How old is this house anyway?"

"At least a hundred years old," I said. "It's a mess, isn't it?"

Addie nodded. "Kind of."

"My parents call it a fixer-upper," I said. The old floorboards squeaked under my feet. "You'd never know my parents worked on it for weeks before we moved in."

"I guess it'll be really nice someday," Addie said, brushing a clump of dust from her orange pants. "Right now it really does look like a creepy old house from a horror movie."

"Tell me about it," I sighed. "Actually, the best

thing about this house is that it's enormous. There are so many rooms, I'll be able to get away from Peter and my parents. I'll have my own space." Our old house on the other side of town was really tiny.

"Let me see your room," Addie said. She started up the stairs.

"Don't lean too hard on the banister," I warned. "It's kind of creaky."

I started after her, but stopped. "Oh, wait. Someone left the basement door open. I don't want the cat to go down there."

Addie was halfway up the stairs. "What's in the basement?"

"Who knows? I haven't gone down yet. It's too dark and it smells like someone died down there."

I trotted down the hall and stopped at the open basement door. It creaked as I started to close it.

I froze when I heard another sound. A moan?

Who could be down there?

I held my breath and listened. I heard a soft scraping sound. Like shoes against concrete. Footsteps?

Grabbing the doorframe, I leaned forward and peered down the stairs. Dark. So dark I couldn't see where the stairs ended.

I heard another muffled moan. So soft. As if from far away. More shoes scraping across the concrete floor.

"Hey—is anyone there?" I tried the light switch. I clicked it once, twice, three times. Nothing happened.

"Peter? Is that you?" I called. My voice sounded hollow in the heavy darkness of the stairwell. "Peter?"

"What? Are you calling me, Danielle?" Peter shouted from the kitchen. "Mom and I are unpacking!"

Okay. So it wasn't Peter.

I leaned farther into the darkness. "Dad? Are you home?" I called. My voice cracked. "Dad? Is that you down there?"

I listened hard. Silence now.

And then I heard a sigh. Long and low.

More scraping. A soft *thud*.

And then a whisper . . . so soft and distant . . .

A whisper . . .

"Peter . . . we're waiting . . . Peter . . ."

"Who's there?" I called softly. "Who is it?"
Silence now.
"Did someone call my brother's name?"
Silence.
"I'm coming down there!" I threatened.
Silence.
I listened hard for another few seconds. Then I slammed the basement door shut. I pressed my back against it and struggled to catch my breath.

There's no one in the basement, I told myself. *You didn't hear that.*

All old houses make noises—all kinds of creaks and groans and sighs.

And whispers.

Everyone knows that.

I told myself I was just freaked out about moving, about moving into this huge, creepy house. I told myself that I was just hearing things.

But I had to find out for sure. So I took a deep breath, pushed away from the door, turned, and started to pull it open once again.

"Hey!" I cried out when the door wouldn't budge. "Hey!"

I twisted the heavy brass doorknob and tugged. Then I twisted it the other way. I took another deep breath and tugged with both hands, groaning loudly as I pulled.

Stuck. The door was completely stuck now.

"Danielle." Mom's voice startled me. I jumped. She staggered past, struggling under the weight of a big moving carton. "Did Addie leave already?"

"Uh . . . no," I replied. I opened my mouth to tell Mom about the whisper in the basement but decided against it. She would just tell me to take ten deep breaths and calm down. "Addie is still upstairs," I said. "I haven't started the house tour."

I hurried to join her.

I found Addie at the end of the hall outside my parents' room. She had her arms crossed in front of her and was staring hard at a framed photograph on the wall.

"Do you believe that's the first thing my parents hung up in the new house?" I said, a little breathless from running up the stairs.

Addie squinted harder. "What *is* it?"

"It's Peter's old teddy bear," I replied.

"But . . . *why?*" Addie asked.

"You know. They think everything Peter does is adorable." I rubbed a finger down the glass over the photograph. "Peter started wearing glasses when he was really tiny. He had some kind of eye muscle defect, and so he had to wear these tiny glasses. Everyone called him the Little Professor. Adorable, right?"

"Adorable," Addie echoed.

"Well, one day Peter toddles into my parents' room. He's put the glasses on the teddy bear. He holds up the bear, and he says, "Look! Now Teddy can see how cute I am!'"

Addie laughed.

"Okay. It's kind of amusing," I said. "But my parents went berserk, gushing about how wonderful Peter was. And they started crying their eyes out."

"Wow," Addie murmured.

"Do you believe it? They thought it was the cutest thing they ever saw. And then my dad took this picture of the teddy bear with the little glasses on so they'd never forget the moment."

Addie gazed at the photo for a few more seconds, then turned to me with a smile on her face. "I think it's a sweet story, Danielle."

I stuck my finger down my throat and made loud gagging sounds.

"I think you're jealous," she said.

I exploded. "Who, me? Jealous of that creep? Could you possibly say anything stupider?"

She raised both hands in surrender. "Okay, okay. I didn't mean it. Show me your room."

I felt bad. I didn't want to fight with my best friend. Besides, Addie never fights with anyone. She will always back down and apologize rather than get into any kind of argument.

I showed her my room. I didn't realize how drab it was until I brought Addie into it. The walls were gray and the carpet was a darker gray.

Outside, the sun had disappeared behind heavy clouds, making the room even darker. The only color anywhere was Addie's bright clothes.

"I . . . I'm going to brighten it up a bit," I said. "You know. Put up a lot of posters and stuff."

I could see Addie struggling to think of something cheerful to say. "It's a nice room for holding seances," she said finally.

I laughed. "You're not still into that weird 'talking-to-the-spirits' stuff, are you?"

Before she could answer, I heard voices outside. Boys' voices.

I ran to the window and peered down to the front yard. The glass was so dust-smeared, I could barely see. But I recognized two guys from our class, Zack Wheeling and Mojo Dyson, jogging up the front walk.

"Hey! I don't believe it!" Addie exclaimed, right behind me. She moved instantly to the dresser mirror and began fixing her ponytail, checking herself out.

The truth was, she and I had major crushes on *both* those guys. "What are they *doing* here?" Addie asked. "Did you invite them or something?"

"No way," I said, leaning into the mirror, rubbing a dust smudge off my cheek and pushing my hair back into place.

By the time Addie and I came downstairs, Peter had already opened the door and was welcoming the two boys. "Is that your real name? Mojo?"

From halfway down the stairs, I could see Mojo turn red. That's just his thing. If you talk to him, he blushes. Some kids are like that. I guess they have really sensitive skin or something.

"No. It's not my real name," he told Peter.

"What's your real name?" Peter demanded.

Mojo turned a darker red. "Not saying."

Peter wouldn't quit. He never does. "Why not? Is it something really dumb? Like Archibald?"

Mojo and Zack laughed. "How'd he guess your real name, Archibald?" Zack said.

"Hi, Archibald!" Addie called.

The guys looked up and saw us for the first time.

"Hey," Zack said, giving us a quick, two-fingered salute. He always gave that salute. "What's up?"

"What are you guys doing here?" I asked. It didn't come out quite the way I meant it.

"We brought you a housewarming gift," Mojo said.

"But we ate it on the way over," Zack added, grinning. "Actually, it was two Snickers bars."

"We were kind of hungry," Mojo said.

"Nice," I sighed, rolling my eyes. "Well, this is it." I motioned with one hand. "Our new palace. It's—" Something caught my eye down the hall, and I gasped.

The basement door—it had been jammed shut. Stuck.

Now it stood wide open again.

I turned to Peter. "How did you get the basement door open?"

He frowned. "I didn't. I never touched it."

I stared at the door. "Weird."

"Are you guys going to the game next Friday night?" Addie asked. "Maybe we could hang out or something after?"

Before they could answer, Peter interrupted. "I got a new computer for my birthday. It's all hooked up. Are you into *Tomb Raider*? I have the new one. It's been totally upgraded. And guess what else I got? Next year's *NFL Football*."

Zach let out a little cry. "You've got the new *Tomb Raider*? Is it cool?"

Peter nodded. "Yeah. It's awesome. The graphics are unbelievable."

Mojo slipped an arm around Peter's shoulders. "You're my MAN! Where is it? Let's check it out."

The three boys pushed past Addie and me to get up the stairs to Peter's room. A few seconds later, the door slammed behind them.

Addie and I stood frozen in the front hallway, as if in shock. "What just happened?" Addie asked finally. "Was it something we said?"

"Peter strikes again," I said, rolling my eyes. "I'm serious. Is there any way I can become an only child?"

Two days later, I would feel *very* guilty for saying that.

Two days later, my nightmare started with a knock on the front door.

Sunday morning my parents were getting ready to leave on one of their short business trips. As usual, Mom packed the entire suitcase while Dad decided which neckties to bring.

I was leaning against the doorway to my parents' room, watching Mom pack. Yellow morning sunlight filtered through the window blinds, making stripes on the unmade bed.

Peter kept jumping up and down on the mattress, making their suitcase bounce. "Why can't I come?" he demanded. "Why don't you ever take me with you?"

Mom frowned at him. "There *is* a little thing called school tomorrow," she said softly.

"I can make up the work," Peter insisted. "Why can't I come? Why do I always have to stay home with Danielle? She'll only invite all her friends over and have a party, and tell me to get lost!"

"Whoa, Peter—" I shouted. "That is so untrue!"

Dad narrowed his eyes at me. "Are you having a party tonight?"

"Of course not," I told him, glaring at Peter. Then I added sarcastically, "I'm going to spend all my time taking good care of my sweet little brother."

"I can take care of myself," Peter grunted.

Dad tilted his head, the way he always does when he's thinking hard about something. "Danielle, are you sure you don't want Aunt Kate to come stay over?"

"No way!" I cried. "We don't need her. Really, Dad. I've taken care of Peter before, haven't I?"

"We have to go," Mom said, checking her watch. She slammed the suitcase shut and clasped it. "We'll call you from Cleveland," she told me.

"Hey, wait. You forgot my ties!" Dad cried.

A few minutes later, after hugs and kisses all around, and more promises to call and warnings to be careful, my parents backed down the driveway and headed for the airport.

I watched their car until it disappeared around the corner. Then I turned to Peter. "Help me clean up the breakfast dishes?"

"I can't," he said. "I have to go watch TV." He spun around and ran out of the kitchen.

I let out a sigh. It's going to be a long couple of days, I told myself. Peter is always at his worst when Mom and Dad are away and I'm in charge.

I started carrying the dishes to the sink. And that's when I heard the knock on the front door. Three sharp raps.

At first, I thought Mom and Dad had returned. They probably forgot something.

But why wouldn't they just open the door?

Three more sharp raps.

"Coming!" I shouted. I hurried down the long hall and pulled open the front door.

"Addie!"

She had a purple sweater pulled down over electric blue leggings. Her blond hair fell wild around her face. "I tried the doorbell, but I don't think it works," she said.

"It isn't hooked up," I told her. I stepped back so she could come in. The bright sunlight seemed to follow her into the house.

"My parents just left for the airport. I'm alone here with Peter the Great."

"Fun time," she said. She followed me into the living room.

"What's up?" I asked, gazing at the large book she held in her arms.

"I figured out what we can do, Danielle."

"Huh?"

"You know. For the talent show." She crinkled her nose. And then sneezed. "Is it dusty in here?"

"A little," I said. "My parents have been so busy

18

unpacking, there hasn't been time to dust. What's your big idea for us?"

"Hypnotism," Addie said. Her green eyes flashed with excitement. "I'm going to hypnotize you!"

I took a step back. "You're kidding, right? You don't know anything about hypnotism, and neither do I. Why would I ever let you hypnotize me?"

Addie groaned. "I don't mean I'm *really* going to hypnotize you. We're going to fake it. You know. Pretend. That's why I brought the book."

She held it up so I could read the title: *Hypnotism for Everyone*.

I squinted at her. "You're serious about this, aren't you!"

"This book will tell us how to make it look real," Addie said. "I'll pretend to put you in a trance. And then I'll have you go back, back, back in time, back to your previous lives."

I crossed my arms in front of my chest. "What previous lives?"

"We'll make up something," Addie replied. "It'll be great, Danielle! You'll tell some wild stories about living in the past. The audience will love it. They'll *believe* it!"

I stepped over to the living room window and felt the bright sunlight warm me. On the street, two boys sped by on bikes, chased by a big, yapping dog.

I started to turn back to Addie when something

caught my eye. A man. Half-hidden in the shadows of the twisted old maple tree at the bottom of our front yard.

Who is that? I wondered, feeling a flash of fear.

I squinted to see him better. He leaned away from the tree, and I could see that he wore a black raincoat over black slacks. I couldn't see his face. It was still hidden in the shadows. But I could see him staring, just standing there, hiding behind the gnarled tree trunk, staring up at our house.

Why was he staring at our house? What was he watching for? Who *was* he?

"What's wrong?" Addie asked, stepping up beside me.

"Uh . . . I'll be right back," I said.

My heart pounding, I crossed the room and made my way to the front door. I stuck my head out and squinted into the bright sunlight.

"Hello," I called to the man behind the tree. "Hey."

He didn't answer. A gust of wind made the brown leaves rustle over the ground. All of the old trees in the yard trembled and creaked.

I cupped my hands around my mouth and tried again. "Hello? Can I help you?"

No answer.

Without thinking, I pushed past the storm door and began running toward the tree. It had rained the day before, and my shoes sank into the soft, wet ground. The gusting wind made the dead, brown leaves dance around me.

I hugged myself against the autumn cold. "Hello?"

I stepped into the shadow of the maple tree—and gasped.

No one there.

The man was gone. Vanished.

I took a deep breath.

And two hands grabbed me roughly from behind.

I cried out. And spun free.

"Danielle, what's your problem?" Addie asked.

"You—you scared me to death!" I told her breathlessly. "There was a man—here."

"Huh?" She looked past me to the tree. "What man?"

"I don't know. He—he disappeared. But look—" I pointed to the ground. Deep shoe prints in the wet dirt behind the tree.

"Maybe it was the mailman," Addie said. She put an arm around my shoulders and led me back to the house. "You've been so tense ever since you moved here, Danielle."

I closed the door behind us and bolted it. Addie headed back into the living room. But I had a sudden urge to get out of the house.

"Let's get our bikes and ride up to Summerville Park," I suggested.

Addie shook her head. "No. We have to rehearse. We have to do this hypnotism thing."

I dropped down onto the couch. "Addie, *why* do we have to do this? Why do we have to be in the stupid talent show, anyway?"

She sighed and set the book down on the coffee table. "Because of Zack and Mojo, of course!"

My mouth dropped open. "Huh?"

"Danielle, those guys came over here, and they went right to Peter's room. They think a nine-year-old kid is more interesting than we are!"

She tossed the book aside and plopped down beside me on the couch. "Look. We've been in high school two years, and hardly anyone knows we're there. I want to be noticed. I want kids to say, 'Hey, there goes Addie. She and Danielle are really cool.'"

"But, Addie—" I started.

"Don't you want Zack and Mojo to think *we're* more interesting than Peter's stupid computer games?" she asked.

"Well, yeah. Sure." Once Addie gets worked up like this, there's no stopping her. "There's also a two-hundred-dollar prize, right?"

"Right."

"Let's do it," I said.

"Excellent!" She picked up the hypnotism book. "This is going to be a great act. We'll make it look so real that—"

"Just one thing," I said. "I'll do this crazy act only if I can hypnotize *you*!"

She stared at me. "*You* want to be the hypnotist?"

I nodded.

She thought about it for a few seconds. "Okay. Deal." She laughed. "I've got some *awesome* ideas about my previous lives!"

So we set to work. First we flipped through the book, reading the parts about how to put someone in a trance. It was all pretty much the way I'd seen it on TV and in movies.

"We need a coin," Addie said. "A big, shiny coin."

"I have a silver dollar on a chain," I remembered. "It'll be perfect."

I found the silver dollar in my jewelry box, and we started practicing with it. Addie sat on the couch, and I stood in front of her. I waved the silver dollar slowly back and forth in front of her and said in a soft, calm voice, "You're getting sleepy . . . sleepy. . . . Your eyelids are beginning to feel heavy. . . ."

Addie let her head fall back against the couch and started snoring really loudly.

"Very funny," I groaned. "I thought you wanted to be serious about this."

She opened her eyes and sat up. "Yes. I do. You're doing great, Danielle. That whole coin thing. The way you whispered everything. Terrific. I almost believed it myself."

"Well, let's practice taking you back in time," I

said. "First you have to be a little girl, you know. Then a baby."

"Goo-goo," Addie said in a tiny voice.

I raised the coin and began swinging it slowly again. "Watch the coin," I whispered. "Follow it closely."

"What are you doing?" a voice called from the doorway.

The chain fell from my hand. The coin rattled onto the living room floor and slid toward the door.

Peter darted into the room and grabbed it before I could reach it. "What's this, Danielle? What were you doing?"

"Hypnotizing me," Addie told him. "She's very good at it."

"I'm an expert," I said. "I can put anyone into a trance in seconds."

Peter stared hard at me. "You can really hypnotize people?"

"Of course she can," Addie said. "She can hypnotize anyone."

"Hypnotize me!" Peter demanded.

"No way," I said, reaching for the coin. "Addie and I are too busy."

He swung it out of my grasp. "Hypnotize me, Danielle. I won't give it back to you unless you hypnotize me too!"

"Peter, we're doing this for school," I said. "Give it back!"

Behind his red glasses, his dark eyes flashed excitedly. Waving the coin at me, he began to chant, "Hypnotize me! Hypnotize me! Hypnotize me!"

I grabbed for it again. Missed.

Addie jumped up beside me. "Okay. Let's hypnotize him," she said. "Why not?"

I turned to her. "Excuse me?"

"Go ahead. Put him in a trance. Turn him into a chicken or a puppy or something."

"Yeah! Turn me into a puppy!" Peter cried. He let out a loud cheer. "Go ahead. Hypnotize me. This is so cool!"

I grabbed the silver dollar away from him. "I'll do it if you promise one thing, Peter. After I'm finished hypnotizing you, you have to promise to leave Addie and me alone and not pester us."

"No problem," he said. "Where do I sit?"

I pushed him toward the couch. "Sit down there. Lean back. Get comfortable. You have to relax if I'm going to put you in a trance."

Peter leaped onto the couch. He bounced up and down several times on the cushion.

"What are you doing?" I snapped.

"This is how I relax," he said. Then he stopped bouncing, and his face grew serious. "Danielle, am I going to feel weird?"

"You won't feel a thing," I told him. "You'll be in a trance, remember?"

I knew exactly what I was going to do. I was going

26

to do my coin routine, swing it back and forth. Then I would pretend to put him in a trance.

Of course, Peter would say he didn't feel anything. It didn't work. And then I planned to tell him it was because he was in such a deep trance, he just didn't remember.

What a shame it didn't work out the way I had imagined.

"Come on, sit still, Peter." I pushed him till his head rested on the couch back. "And don't talk."

Addie had wandered over to the front window. She sat on the window ledge with her arms crossed over her purple sweater, fiddling with her glass beads, watching us.

Outside, the sunlight faded in and out. Shadows seemed to reach up and swallow Addie.

I turned back to Peter. "Keep your eye on the coin," I said. Holding the chain high, I began to swing the silver dollar. "Follow the coin. . . . Follow it closely. . . ." I whispered.

Peter burst out laughing.

"What's so funny?" I snapped.

"You are," he said. "You're a total fake, aren't you?"

"Of course she isn't," Addie chimed in. "We both studied that hypnotism book." She pointed to the book on the table beside the couch. "We've been practicing for weeks, Peter."

Peter stared at the book. "Really?"

I sighed. "I can't hypnotize you if you keep laughing and asking questions."

Peter pushed his glasses up on his nose. "Well, what are you going to do to me when I'm hypnotized?"

"I'm going to make you remember things you've forgotten," I told him. "And then we'll see if you have any past lives."

"Cool," he said. He settled back. "Do it."

Addie flashed me a thumbs-up. I raised the silver dollar and turned back to Peter. "Watch the coin, Peter," I whispered. "You're getting very sleepy . . . very sleepy. . . ."

He didn't burst out laughing this time. He didn't say a word. His expression was solemn. He rested his head against the back of the couch, and nothing moved but his eyes. Back and forth . . . slowly, so slowly . . . back and forth.

"You feel so drowsy now, Peter. Your eyelids feel heavy . . . so heavy. . . . You can barely keep them open. . . ."

Perched on the window ledge, Addie shifted her weight. She seemed to fade deeper into the shadows.

"Sleepy . . . so sleepy . . . " I whispered. "Your legs are asleep. . . . Your arms are asleep. . . . Close your eyes, Peter. . . . Close them now."

Peter obediently closed his eyes. I expected him to burst out laughing, or shout "BOO!" or something.

Instead, a long breath escaped his throat, and his head slumped forward.

Addie laughed. "Your brother is such a good actor," she whispered.

I lowered the coin and stared at my brother. A smile crossed my face. It was totally cute how he was playing along, pretending to be hypnotized.

His eyes were shut tight. He was slumped on the couch, his head tilted forward. He was taking slow, steady breaths.

"When I snap my fingers, you will come out of the trance," I said. I snapped my fingers.

Peter didn't move.

I snapped my fingers again. "That's the signal for you to open your eyes," I said. "You will come out of the trance and feel totally normal."

Peter didn't move. As he breathed, so slowly and softly, his chin bobbed on his chest.

I snapped my fingers again. Then I hit my hands together in a sharp clap.

He didn't open his eyes. Or jump up. Or anything. In fact, his breathing seemed to get slower, softer.

"Okay, Peter. Cut the joke," I groaned.

"Yeah. Forget about it! Enough already," Addie said. "You're starting to scare us."

"This is so not funny, Peter," I said. I leaned over him and clapped my hands right in his ear.

He didn't react at all. Didn't flinch. Didn't move.

Addie and I frowned at each other. "Come on, Peter," I pleaded. "Get up. You promised you'd let Addie and me practice."

"It isn't funny," Addie said. "We know you're faking. We know you're not really in a trance."

Peter's head bobbed steadily on his chest. His eyes didn't open.

My throat suddenly felt tight and dry. My legs were trembling. "Peter, it's not a good joke," I said. "Stop it. Just stop it, okay? Open your eyes and get going!"

He didn't move. His steady breaths—whoosh . . . whoosh . . . whoosh—suddenly sounded deafening to me.

"What are we going to do?" I gasped.

"Tickle him," Addie suggested. "That'll wake him up!"

"Yes!" I cried. "Peter is totally ticklish."

I plunged both hands into his ribs and started to tickle. His head bounced around lifelessly. His eyes remained shut. His mouth dropped open, but he didn't laugh.

I tickled harder. Harder. I dug my fingers into his sides, so hard I knew I was hurting him.

"Wake up!" I screamed. "Peter, wake up!"

"Open your eyes, please!" Addie begged. She had her hands clasped tightly in front of her as if praying. I saw tears in her eyes. "Please, Peter, please!"

And then I had my hands on both of his shoulders, and I was shaking him. Shaking him. Shaking him.

And screaming. Screaming without even hearing myself.

"He won't wake up! What are we going to do? What are we going to DO?"

I shook Peter frantically, screaming his name. His head bobbed limply on his shoulders. His mouth hung open, his tongue falling from side to side.

He suddenly seemed so frail and tiny.

"Peter, please! Peter!"

I suddenly pictured him as a baby. He was such a cute baby with that red hair and tiny freckles all over his face. I pictured him as a toddler, walking unsteadily, peering out at us through his tiny eyeglasses.

"Peter, wake up! I'm sorry! I'm so sorry!"

What have I done?

I gasped when his eyes opened. Slowly, like a doll's eyes when you tilt her straight up. He blinked. He shut them again.

"Peter! Peter! Are you awake?"

Addie and I were both leaning over him, screaming at him.

His eyelids slowly raised. He gazed up at us with

33

a blank, glassy stare. His mouth closed slowly, and he swallowed noisily.

I let go of his shoulders and dropped back a step. "Peter?"

A low groan escaped his open mouth. A sound I'd never heard before. An animal groan from deep inside him. Not a human groan.

He shook his head hard, as if trying to clear his mind. Then he gazed up at Addie and me again, a glassy doll's stare.

Addie squeezed my hand. Her hand was wet and cold as ice. "He's okay, Danielle," she said in a trembling voice. "He's going to be okay."

I slid my hand from hers and swept it gently through Peter's hair. "Peter?" I whispered. "You okay?"

The reply came from deep in his throat. "Unnn-huh." A low grunt. He pulled himself up slowly, still blinking, and shook his head again.

A chill tightened the back of my neck. "Peter, I'm sorry," I choked out. "The hypnotism thing . . . it . . . it was just a joke. I didn't realize . . . " My voice caught in my throat.

"You're okay, right?" Addie asked him. "You feel okay?"

He shifted his weight on the couch and gazed around the room. "I guess," he said finally. And then he asked a question that sent a cold stab through my heart. "Where am I?"

"We—we're in the living room," I stammered.

He took off his glasses and rubbed his eyes. Then he squinted up at me. "The living room? Really?"

Addie uttered a cry. "Stop kidding around, Peter. It isn't funny. You're starting to scare us."

Peter swallowed again. He blinked several times and gazed around. His eyes finally locked on me. "You're Danielle?"

"Yes!" I cried. "Don't you remember me?" I turned to Addie, my whole body shaking in panic. "I don't think he's kidding. I really don't think he remembers," I whispered. "I think I ruined his memory or something."

"No, you didn't," Addie insisted. "You couldn't. You don't even know how to hypnotize someone, Danielle."

"But look at him!" I whispered through my gritted teeth. "He doesn't know where he is! He's totally lost!"

"Hey, you know Peter. He's faking it," she said. "I think he's playing a really cruel joke."

We both turned back to Peter. He stood up shakily and took a few steps, as if testing his legs. Then he stretched his arms over his head. He gazed from Addie to me, concentrating hard, as if trying to remember.

"Should I call Dr. Ross?" I asked him. "Peter? Do you think you need a doctor?"

He squinted at me. He was always so quick.

Mom calls him Motormouth. But now it took him a long time to answer. "I'm . . . fine," he whispered.

He rubbed his forehead and gazed around the room again. "You're Addie. Right?" he asked.

Addie nodded solemnly. "Yes. Right."

"Addie and Danielle," Peter mumbled.

"I think I'd better call Dr. Ross," I said. I reached for the phone beside the couch.

Peter grabbed my arm. "No. I'm fine. I'm okay. Really, Danielle." He let out a short laugh. "I'm just kidding. You know."

I stared hard into his eyes, studying him.

He made a face at me. He stuck out his teeth, crossed his eyes, and made his monkey face. The face that always cracks Mom and Dad up.

Then he laughed. "Stop staring at me like that. I'm fine. Really. I'm perfectly okay. What's wrong with you two?"

Addie and I exchanged glances.

"I'm fine. I'll show you!" Peter cried. He started jumping up and down on the couch cushions. Then he leapt to the floor and did a wild tap dance. "See?"

Addie and I both laughed. "I think he's definitely back to normal," Addie said.

I still felt shaky. "Peter, you remember where you are now? You remember our names?"

"Duh," he said.

"He's back to normal," Addie sighed.

Then his expression changed. "Did you really hypnotize me?" he asked suddenly. "I felt kinda weird for a little while. Kinda dizzy or something."

"I—I don't know what happened," I told him. "But I'm glad you're okay. You're not dizzy now, are you?"

He shook his head. "I feel great."

"Then you can go," I said. "Addie and I have to practice our act."

"Why can't I hang out with you?" he asked.

"Peter, you promised," I said.

"I'll be quiet. Really," he insisted. "You won't even know I'm here. Please please please?"

Addie rolled her eyes. "He's definitely back to normal."

I gave Peter a shove toward the front stairs. "Out of here. You promised you'd leave us alone if I hypnotized you. Now, beat it."

He grumbled some more. Then he headed up to his room, taking the stairs two at a time, slapping the banister loudly with each step.

I turned and saw that Addie was at the front door. "I'd better go," she said. "That was kind of weird. I know you don't feel like rehearsing our act now."

"I never want to hypnotize anyone again," I said, shaking my head. "Even if it's pretend."

"That's just it," Addie said. "It was pretend, Danielle. You couldn't have hypnotized your brother. You couldn't."

37

"Then what happened to him?" I asked.

Addie frowned. "I . . . I don't know," she murmured. "At least he snapped out of it. That was scary for a minute or two. Hey, I'll call you later." She hurried out.

I closed the door after her. Then I just stood in the hallway trembling. I couldn't get that horrifying picture of Peter out of my mind—sprawled there so lifelessly as I shook him and shook him.

"Get it together," I scolded myself. "Everything is fine now."

I took a deep breath, pushed that picture from my mind, forced myself to move. Gripping the banister tightly, I pulled myself up the stairs, then down the long hallway to Peter's room.

The door was closed. I leaned close and pressed my ear against the door.

Silence in there.

My heart began to race.

Why was it so quiet in there? Was he really okay? Peter was never quiet.

I raised my fist and knocked on the door, harder than I had intended. "Peter? It's me."

No reply.

"Peter?"

I pounded again. Still no answer. So I twisted the knob and pushed open the door. "Peter—?"

He was sitting in front of his computer with his back to me. The computer was on, the monitor screen flashing bright colors and the name of the game, *Tomb Raider*. No sound. He had a game controller gripped in one hand.

I took a few steps into the room. "Peter? Didn't you hear me?"

He turned slowly. The red and yellow lights from the monitor screen reflected eerily in his glasses. I couldn't see his eyes.

"Peter—?"

"Hi," he said finally.

The words *Tomb Raider* blinked on the screen in huge letters, red, then green, then blue. The colors washed over Peter's face.

"Are you feeling okay?" I asked.

"Yeah. I told you. I'm fine," he snapped. "How many times do I have to say it?"

"Sorry," I murmured.

"Can I just ask you a question, Danielle?"

"Yes, of course," I said. "What is it?"

"How do you play this game?"

I gasped. *Tomb Raider* was his favorite game. Why couldn't he remember how to play it?

He sat there gazing at me, the colors dancing over his face, twisting the controller in his hand. "Do you know how to start it?" he asked softly.

I forced myself not to cry out. I held my breath. I tried not to panic.

I had never played the game, but I knew I could figure out how to get it started. Leaning over him, I moved the controller. After fumbling around for a minute or two, I got the game to start. I picked the beginner level, even though I knew Peter was an expert player.

Peter took the controller and started to play. I watched him, my heart pounding hard, my arms crossed tightly in front of me.

"Hey, this is too easy!" he cried. He moved the controller until the setup screen returned. "You jerk. You set it for Beginner," he growled. "I'm not a beginner. I've already beaten this game three times!"

He started the game again, leaning into the monitor. The colors danced over his face as if he were in the game.

He didn't even seem to remember that I was standing there. I tiptoed out of the room.

Is he okay or not? I asked myself.

Should I call Dr. Ross?

One minute he's asking me how to start a game he's played a million times. The next minute, he's an expert again. . . .

"What have I done? What have I done?" I repeated in a whisper.

I decided I'd better call the doctor.

My hand shook as I punched in the phone number and listened to the ringing at the other end.

After four rings, a taped message began. No one in the doctor's office. Of course. It was Sunday. I shut the phone off and tossed it onto the couch. As it hit the couch, it rang.

I jumped. What if it's Mom and Dad?

What do I tell them? That everything is fine? Or do I tell them what I did? Tell them how weird Peter is acting?

I stared at the phone. It rang again. Again.

Finally, my heart thudding, I grabbed it. "Hello?" My voice came out tiny and shrill.

"Hey, Danielle?"

"Who is this?"

"It's me. Zack."

I couldn't help myself. I burst out laughing. I guess I was so relieved that it wasn't my parents.

"What's so funny?" he asked. He sounded hurt.

"Nothing," I said quickly. "It's . . . been a little weird around here today." I dropped onto the couch. "What's up, Zack?"

"Did your parents go away?" he asked.

"Uh . . . yeah. They're on their way to Cleveland."

"Well, I thought maybe you and I could grab a hamburger or something."

Hel-lo. Zack was asking me out? How great was that? But why today of all days?

"I'd really like to," I said. "But I don't know. I'm in charge of Peter. I can't go out and leave him alone."

"Bring him," Zack declared. "He's pretty cool, your brother. Why don't you bring him?"

"Well . . . yes! Great! Hold on. I'll go ask him."

I dropped the phone and ran back up to my brother's room. He was still leaning over his computer, frantically playing the game.

"Peter, would you like to come have dinner with Zack and me tonight?" I asked, shouting over the game.

He kept playing for a few seconds, then put the game on pause. He turned slowly. "What?"

"Would you like to go to dinner with Zack and me?" I asked. "You know. Go to Burger Palace or something?"

"Cool!" he cried. He jumped to his feet. "When are we going? Now? I'm starving!"

I burst out laughing. That was the same old Peter! He'd do anything to hang out with my friends.

I had a big smile on my face as I hurried back to the phone to tell Zack we had a date.

Burger Palace was noisy and jammed with people, even though it was a Sunday night. The three of us found a booth in the back. Zack and I slid in on one side. Peter playfully tried to shove into the same side.

"Get over there!" I cried, pushing him out. "You're not funny."

He laughed and moved to the other side of the table. Then he picked up the menu—upside down—and pretended to read it.

Normally, Peter's stunts to get attention drive me crazy. But tonight I was so thrilled to see him acting like himself, I didn't care if he stood on his head on the table!

"This was an excellent idea," I told Zack. We started to talk about school and kids we knew. I realized I really liked Zack. I wondered if he really liked me too.

Of course, Peter kept butting into the conversation. He had about a dozen dumb jokes that he insisted on telling.

But I didn't get tense about it. I sat back and enjoyed myself.

I felt so good. So relaxed.

So relieved.

I stayed in a good mood until the food came.

Then I stared across the table at my brother. I stared with growing horror as he picked up French fries and stuffed them into his mouth, then picked up his double cheeseburger.

"Peter—!" I gasped. "What are you doing?"

He gazed at me, chewing hard. "Huh? What's wrong?"

"You—you're right-handed," I said. "Why are you eating with your left hand?"

Mom and Dad called a few minutes after we returned home.

"Hi." I knew it was them before I answered.

"We're in the car, on the way to the hotel," Mom said. "Is everything okay, Danielle?"

I opened my mouth to tell them that everything wasn't okay. Come home, quick. I accidentally hypnotized Peter and now he isn't the same. I cast some kind of spell on him, and he's acting totally weird.

But I couldn't tell them. I couldn't. Besides, I knew they wouldn't believe me. Who would believe a crazy story like that?

"Fine," I said. "Everything is fine, Mom."

We talked for a minute or so. I told her we went to Burger Palace for dinner. Mom said something, but I couldn't hear very well. The connection kept cutting out.

I told her Peter was up in his room doing homework for tomorrow. She didn't seem to hear me. "Peter is fine," I lied.

"Who?" The phone crackled with static.

"Peter," I repeated.

"I can't hear you," Mom shouted. "I'd better get off. We'll be home tomorrow night."

Then silence. The connection was lost.

When I clicked off the phone, I was shaking. I hate lying to my parents. But what choice did I have?

Peter will be normal again by the time they return home tomorrow night, I told myself. Mom and Dad will never have to know.

Late that night I couldn't sleep. I stared up at the cracks in my ceiling and thought about Peter. Maybe he's still hypnotized, I thought. Maybe if I go up to him and snap my fingers or something, I can bring him out of it.

Or maybe I can try to hypnotize him again and—

My mind spun. I couldn't stop thinking about it. I felt so helpless. I didn't know what to do.

I grabbed my pillow and pulled it over my face. I tried to shut out the dim moonlight from outside, shut out the ceiling cracks above my head, shut out my troubled thoughts.

Finally, I fell into a light, restless sleep. I slept until the whispers started. So soft and distant, at first I thought they were part of a dream.

Tiny voices, speaking so quietly. Sighing. Moaning.

I struggled to hear them. What were they whispering?

"Who's there?" I cried, my voice tight, clogged with sleep.

I swung my feet to the floor and clicked on the bedside table lamp. Was I dreaming? Or were the whispers coming from down the hall?

Shivering, I stood unsteadily. "Who—who's there?" I repeated.

Burglars? Had someone broken in?

"Who's there?"

I stumbled to the doorway and peered up and down the dark hall. No one. Peter's door was closed. No light from under it.

And then the whispers began again. "Peter . . . Peter . . . "

I gasped. Was someone calling my brother?

It couldn't be a burglar. A burglar wouldn't be calling Peter.

The whispers seemed to float up the front stairway.

I clicked on the hall light, tugged down the hem of my nightshirt, and ran to the top of the stairs. "Who is it?"

"Peter . . ."

"Please! Who's there?"

My heart thudding, I raced down the stairs, the wood cold on my bare feet. My hand fumbled on the wall, finally pushing the switch, and the living room lights flickered on.

I gazed around the empty room.

"Peter . . . we're waiting. . . ."

"Who's here? Is someone in here?" I didn't recognize my shrill, frightened voice.

Danielle, call the police! I ordered myself.

I started to the phone. But I stopped when I saw the door open. The door to the basement stairs. Wide-open again, even though I had carefully closed it before going to bed.

Shivering, I hugged my nightshirt around me. Slowly, I made my way down the hall to the open door.

"Peter . . . "

I grabbed the door and peered into the darkness of the basement stairs. "Who's there?" I shouted in a quivering voice. "Please! Who is it? Who?"

"Peter . . . Peter . . ."

The whispers were so faint, so pleading. As if they were calling to him, begging him to come down.

Who was down there?

I took a deep breath, struggling to force my body to stop trembling. Then I reached into the stairwell and clicked on the basement light.

Darkness.

Oh. I remembered. The switch was broken.

"Peter . . . Peter . . ."

I grabbed the heavy metal flashlight off its hook on the wall. I clicked it on and sent a beam of white light down the stairs. The light bounced over the plaster basement wall below. The steps were steep and crooked, tilted one way and another.

I took another deep breath, then stepped into the stairwell. I swept the light down the stairs, then over the basement floor.

No one there.

The whispers stopped. Damp, heavy air floated

up to greet me, sour smelling and musty. I gripped the flashlight so tightly my hand ached.

"I—I'm coming down," I shouted.

Silence.

I'll stop at the bottom, I decided. If I see someone, I'll run back upstairs and call the police.

Gripping the flashlight in one hand, pressing my other hand against the cold plaster wall, I slowly made my way down. Step-by-step. The stairs groaned beneath my weight. I could feel thick dust collecting on the soles of my bare feet.

The light trembled over the basement wall. As I reached the last step, it cracked under my foot. I grabbed the wall to keep from falling.

Stopping to catch my breath, I stared into the circle of trembling white light, and listened.

Silence. Such a heavy silence. Heavy as the damp, stale air.

And then I heard a moan.

I gasped.

Should I turn and run back up?

"Anyone here?" I tried to shout, but the words escaped in a whisper.

I swept the beam of light around the basement. I could see a large, low-ceilinged room, cluttered with cartons, old wardrobes, a battered dresser and other furniture, a stack of folding chairs, cans and jars, old newspapers piled nearly to the ceiling. . . .

Then . . . then . . . *a human figure*! A figure standing

stiffly in an empty square of bare floor. He had his back to me. He wore a dark jacket, collar raised, over black pants. At first, I thought it was a mannequin or clothing dummy.

But then he moved.

Captured in the light, he turned slowly. A boy with long, black hair. He raised a bony hand and pointed at me with a slender finger.

"Ohhh," I whispered. The flashlight started to slip from my hand. And as the light swerved, I saw another figure. A girl standing stiffly beside him. She wore a dark T-shirt over baggy jeans. Her blond hair spiked out around her face.

A wave of panic made my legs tremble. I grasped the flashlight tightly. "Who—who are you?" I choked out.

My hand shook. In the quivering light, I saw another boy, short and chubby with his hands raised to his cheeks. And another boy, pointing another bony finger at me.

"*Peter . . . Peter . . .* " they chanted. The four of them. The four strange intruders in my basement.

"Who are you? What are you *doing* down here?" I screamed.

They moved forward. Huddled side by side, they took a step toward me. My light trembled over their faces. Their glowing, shimmering faces.

"No—!" I cried out as I saw why they shimmered so eerily.

Their skin . . . their hands and arms . . . their faces . . . covered by a thick goo. A shimmering, clear slime. Like a clear, wet gelatin.

Their hair glowed in the thick layer of slime. It stretched over their wide-open eyes. Over their entire heads. They were trapped inside it.

And as they opened their mouths to whisper my brother's name, the gelatin bubbled, then snapped back tight.

"Peter . . . Peter . . ."

Trapped inside their clear cocoons, they moved in unison, slowly like robots—like *zombies*—they took another step toward me.

"This isn't happening," I murmured out loud.

Their eyes stared coldly at me through the thick, wet layer of jelly.

I spun away. Started to run to the stairs.

But another figure caught my eye. Another dark figure, standing behind the four terrifying kids. Hunched over as if in pain. Standing so still . . .

My whole body shuddered in terror. The four shimmering kids took another slow step toward me. I raised the light to the boy hunched behind them. It washed over his pale face, his wide, staring eyes, his mouth open in a silent cry.

And I screamed in horror.

"PETER!"

"Peter . . . Peter . . ."

Chanting through the bubbling film that covered them, the four kids reached out for me. I saw their unblinking, lifeless eyes. Grasping hands.

Grabbing for me. Mucus-covered hands, bony fingers grasping . . .

"Peter . . . Peter . . ."

Behind them, Peter stood still, as if frozen to the spot. His dark eyes glared from behind his glasses, so sad and frightening at the same time.

I dropped the flashlight. It hit my bare foot, shooting pain up my leg. Then it clattered onto the hard floor, making the beam of light roll crazily over the wall.

I spun away with another scream. Spun away, grabbed the flashlight, and started to run.

Before I realized it, I was up the stairs. Their eerie chant rang in my ears: *"Peter . . . Peter . . ."*

I pictured their grasping hands, their eyes so dead, so dead behind the covering of slime.

Panting hard, I burst through the doorway. I slammed the door hard. Slammed it and pushed my shoulder against it.

And listened. Listened to my wheezing breaths, my thudding heartbeat.

And then I was running through the dimly lit living room. To the stairs. And racing up the stairs, my side aching, each breath feeling as if my lungs would burst.

Into my room. Into bed. Into the silent, safe darkness.

Safe?

I sat up, still trembling, trembling so hard my teeth chattered.

"It was a dream," I told myself, my voice shaking too. "Danielle, you're safe in your own bed. You never went downstairs. It was a dream. It had to be a dream."

I hugged myself hard, staring at the gray light washing in through the bedroom window.

All a dream . . .

Of course. A dream.

I stood up, still hugging myself. I'll prove it, I decided. I can prove it was all a dream. I will go into Peter's room, and he will be sleeping soundly, tucked in, sleeping peacefully in his own bed.

Peter safe and sound, asleep in his bed. Not in

the basement with those creatures from my nightmare.

I hesitated, gripped with fear. What if Peter wasn't asleep in his room?

What if he was down in the basement with the slime-covered kids?

What would I do then?

What *could* I do?

I took a deep breath and pressed my hand against my chest, as if trying to *force* my heart to stop racing.

Then I took a shaky step toward the hall. My legs felt so rubbery and weak. I was dizzy with fear. The floor tilted and rocked beneath me as I made my way slowly down the long hall toward Peter's room.

I stopped outside his door.

Said a silent prayer.

"Peter, please be in there. Please!"

I turned the knob and pushed open the door. I clicked on the ceiling light.

And blinking in the sudden bright light, I stared at his bed.

Empty.

Peter wasn't there.

I stared in horror at the tangled sheets and blanket. The empty bed.

I heard a sigh. And raised my eyes to the window.

"What are you doing in here?" Peter asked. He was perched on his window seat. His red hair had fallen down over one eye. He wasn't wearing his glasses. One pajama leg was rolled up nearly to his knee.

"Peter, you're here!" I cried happily. I dove across the room and tried to wrap him in a hug. But he dodged away from me.

"Why did you come in here?" he asked, brushing back his hair with one hand.

"I—I—" How could I answer that? "I wanted to make sure you were okay. Why aren't you in bed?"

He shrugged. "Couldn't sleep."

I studied his face. "So you've just been staring out the window?"

He nodded.

"And you weren't down in the basement?" I asked.

"The basement?" He frowned, as if thinking hard about it.

"Were you?" I demanded. "Were you in the basement, Peter?"

"No. Of course not," he said sharply.

And then he startled me. He reached out suddenly and grabbed my wrist.

"Danielle," he whispered through gritted teeth. He squeezed my wrist hard and brought his face close to mine. "Danielle, don't forget me. Please—*don't forget me!*"

The next morning, I dressed for school in a hurry. I gazed out the window as I pulled on a baggy gray sweater over a pair of black straight-legged jeans. It was a cloudy day. Cold, gray light poured into my bedroom, making long, dark shadows over the floor.

Despite the gray, I felt cheerful, eager to get downstairs to breakfast. It was a new day. A new start. My frightening nightmare about the strange, glistening kids was just that—a nightmare.

It's normal to have strange dreams when you move into a new house, I told myself.

And I assured myself that Peter would be okay

today. I guessed that the effects of my dumb spell would be over by now. I guessed that Peter would be his cheerful, talkative, pesty self again.

I guessed wrong.

He stumbled into the kitchen still in his blue striped pajamas. His hair was unbrushed. It stood straight up in back. He squinted at me through his glasses, as if he didn't recognize me.

"Hel-lo," I said. "Aren't you forgetting about a little something? Like school?"

He frowned and rubbed his cheek. "What day is it?"

"Monday," I said. "Here. Pick a cereal. Have your breakfast, then go up and get dressed."

I had pulled three boxes of cereal from the cabinet. But I knew Peter would choose Golden Grahams. That's the only cereal he ever eats.

He walked over to the counter and stared from box to box. "I can't decide," he said softly. And then he turned to me with a heartbreaking, sad, sad expression on his face. And he whispered, "Danielle, which one do I like?"

I bit my bottom lip to keep from crying. "You really don't remember?"

He shook his head.

I picked up the box of Golden Grahams and poured him a bowl. A few minutes later, we sat across from each other at the kitchen counter, gulping down our cereal in silence.

He's lost his memory, I realized, watching him eat with his left hand again. He's forgetting everything. It's much worse today.

What am I going to do? Mom and Dad will be home tonight. And when they see what I've done to my poor brother . . .

A knock on the kitchen door interrupted my terrifying thoughts.

I heard a familiar shout. And saw Addie's smiling face through the window. I pulled open the door and dragged her inside. She was wearing a bright yellow V-neck top over a red T-shirt, and green spandex leggings. "Oh, Addie, I'm so glad to see you!" I exclaimed.

She blinked. "Uh-oh. What's wrong?"

I pointed to Peter at the counter. He had his spoon halfway to his mouth, but he was staring at Addie. Probably trying to remember who she was.

Addie's smile faded quickly. "He isn't any better? He isn't back to normal?"

I shook my head. "He—he's forgetting everything. His memory—"

Addie squeezed my hand. "You must have really hypnotized him, Danielle. By accident."

"I guess," I said. "But I really can't believe that waving a coin back and forth—"

"You must feel so awful," Addie interrupted.

My mouth dropped open. I couldn't hold back. A

59

wave of anger swept over me. "It was all your idea!" I screamed. "You brought the stupid book. You told me to go ahead and hypnotize my brother!"

"But—but—" Addie sputtered.

"Oh, wait!" I cried. "And something else. I was thinking about this all last night. After I hypnotized Peter and he wouldn't wake up, do you remember what you said to him?"

"Huh? Me?" Addie cried. "What? What did I say?"

"I remember it so clearly. You said, 'It's not funny. Forget about it. Enough already.' That's what you said, Addie. *'Forget about it!'*"

Her green eyes flashed. "So? So what?"

"Well—that's what he did!" I screeched. "He forgot about it. He—he listened to you, Addie. And when he woke up, he forgot just about everything!"

She let out an angry cry. "You're really blaming me? Because I said *forget about it*? It's all my fault? Danielle, have you gone crazy?"

"I—I don't know!" I wailed. "I don't know what happened, and I don't know what to do. I'm sorry, Addie. I really am. But I—I'm in a total panic. I'm so afraid!"

"Well, let's just try to *undo* it then," Addie said through gritted teeth. She stomped toward the living room. "Where's the book I left here?"

"Huh? Why? What are you going to do?" I asked, chasing after her.

"Since it's *all my fault*," Addie said bitterly, "I'm going to help fix things. We're going to hypnotize him again. Do exactly what you did yesterday. Then when he's under the spell, I'll tell him to *remember* everything. Then we'll bring him out of it, and he'll be fine."

I realized my heart was pounding. "Do you really think—?"

"Yes. Definitely," Addie said. She gave me a shove. "Hurry. Get the book. We'll be a little late to school, but no big deal. When we're finished, your brother will be his normal, adorable self."

"Peter, you're going to be okay!" I cried.

I turned to the kitchen counter. "Peter?"

He was gone.

"Where did he go?" I gasped.

Addie blinked hard, staring at the empty kitchen stool.

I spun toward the doorway—and saw that the basement door was open again. "Peter?" I ran out into the hall and looked down the stairs. "Peter? What are you doing?"

He was halfway down the stairs, walking so slowly in the dark, a step and then another step.

"Peter? Can't you hear me?" I screamed. "What are you doing? Where are you going?"

Finally he turned back. He stared up at me. Even in the dim light, I could see the confusion on his face.

"Peter, come back up here," I demanded. "Hurry. Why were you going down to the basement?"

"I—I don't know." His voice was flat, faint, as if he were half-asleep. He obediently began climbing back up, slowly, his eyes locked on mine. It seemed to take him forever.

When he finally stepped back into the hallway, I slammed the basement door shut. I wished it had a lock. A chill ran down my back. I remembered those frightening kids in my dream, chanting his name over and over.

Or *was* it a dream?

Were there *ghosts* down there? Monster kids living in the basement? Zombies like in some horror movie?

Crazy thoughts. Really crazy.

But why was Peter heading down there?

I placed my hands gently on his shoulders and

guided him to the living room. "Addie and I are going to help you," I said softly. "You're going to be fine again."

I led him to the couch. I made him sit exactly where he sat the last time.

"Here's the coin," Addie said, handing it to me. "I found it in your room."

My hand shook so hard, I dropped it. It rolled under the coffee table. I bent to pick it up.

"What are you going to do?" Peter asked.

"I'm going to hypnotize you again," I said.

Peter squinted at me. "Again?"

"You're going to be fine," Addie told him, forcing herself to sound cheerful. "You're going to remember everything."

I climbed to my feet and held the chain up. The coin dangled in front of me, catching the light from the front window. *Please work!* I prayed silently. *Please let me return Peter to normal.*

"Sit back, Peter," I instructed. "Take a deep breath and relax." I began to swing the silver dollar gently back and forth.

Peter slumped back on the couch. His eyes followed the coin from left to right, right to left.

"You're starting to feel sleepy," I whispered. "So sleepy. You can hardly keep your eyelids open." I let the coin swing slowly. Peter's eyelids drooped. "You feel so sleepy . . . so sleepy. . . ."

I glimpsed Addie out of the corner of my eye. She

had a tight grin on her face. She flashed me a thumbs-up. "It's working," she whispered.

"No, it isn't," Peter said.

"Huh?" I gasped.

"I don't feel sleepy at all. You're just making me dizzy, swinging that dumb coin back and forth." He started to stand up.

"No, Peter—" I protested. "Let's keep trying. Please—?"

He shook his head. "It isn't working, Danielle. You don't know how to do it."

I turned to Addie. "I'm doing everything the same. What's wrong? Why isn't it working?"

She sighed. "I'm really sorry. Maybe we should go to school."

"Yes," Peter agreed, pushing his glasses up on his nose. "School."

The coin fell from my hand. I didn't bother to pick it up. "I'll get my backpack," I said.

Can Peter handle school? I wondered. Should I take him to Dr. Ross instead?

I turned toward the hall, and uttered a sharp cry when I saw the basement door—*wide-open again*.

"What is going on around here?" I sighed. I totally lost it. I ran down the hall. Grabbed the door—and slammed it as hard as I could. Then I hurried upstairs, grabbed my backpack, and tore out of the house.

"Hey, wait up!" I called to Addie and Peter, waving

to them. But they had started walking without me, and they were already a block ahead.

The sun was still hidden behind low clouds. The air felt heavy and wet, as if a storm were brewing.

As I started to jog, I heard soft thuds behind me. I turned and saw a figure moving rapidly toward me.

It took me a few seconds to recognize him—the man in the black raincoat. The man all in black. The one who had been staring at our house, spying on us through the front window.

Shadows hid him as he trotted under the tall trees along the street. I couldn't see his face. But keeping in the shadows, he came toward me quickly.

I froze in panic for a second. Then I spun away from him and took off.

The backpack bounced hard on my shoulders. My shoes slipped on the wet grass.

I glanced back and saw him gaining on me. His black raincoat flapped loudly behind him.

"Hey—!" he bellowed angrily. "Hey, you—!"

Who is he? Why is he chasing me? I wondered.

I didn't stop to ask. I raced across the street.

Peter and Addie were only half a block ahead of me now. And the tall brick elementary school came into view ahead of them.

If I can catch up to them, maybe I'll be safe, I thought.

But then I heard a *snap*. My backpack strap flew up. The backpack fell off my shoulder. Hit the ground and bounced in front of me. I nearly stumbled over it.

I dove for it.

Frantic now. Frantic to get away.

Away from the flapping black raincoat. The outstretched arms. The evil face hidden in darkness.

I saw the man lurch into the street. Closing in. Closing in on me.

I grabbed the backpack. Too late.

He was steps away from me.

I was caught.

The blare of a car horn made me jump.

I turned in time to see a large blue van roar into the intersection. The man in black jumped back. He disappeared for a second behind the blur of blue.

It was all the time I needed. I scooped up my backpack and ran.

A few seconds later, I caught up to Addie and Peter. Addie caught the distressed look on my face. She stopped. "Danielle, what's wrong?"

I turned back and pointed. "Th-that man—" I sputtered breathlessly.

My mouth dropped open. He was gone. Vanished.

"Never mind," I said quickly. I didn't want to upset Peter. He was already in such bad shape.

Addie and I led him up the wide stone steps to the elementary school. There were no other kids in sight. We were really late.

I stopped at the door and placed a hand on his shoulder. "You sure you'll be okay?"

He nodded.

I hesitated. Could I leave him here? Was I doing the right thing?

"I'll be okay." He reached for the door handle.

I squeezed his shoulder. "Well . . ." I glanced down the street, feeling a chill of fear, expecting to see the man in the black raincoat waiting for me. But the street was empty.

"I'll meet you right back here after school," I told Peter. "Wait for me right here, okay?"

He nodded. He went inside.

Addie and I watched him through the windows in the door, until he disappeared around a corner.

"He's still not right," I said, biting my bottom lip. "When Mom and Dad get home tonight . . ."

"They'll know what to do," Addie said.

"But they left me in charge, Addie. They left me in charge, and I messed up."

Addie forced a smile. "Hey, look on the bright side, Danielle."

"Huh?" I stared at her. That was so typical Addie. Always cheerful no matter what. Always working hard to cheer everyone else up. "What's the bright side?" I asked.

She thought for a moment. "I don't know," she

answered finally. "I guess you should just try not to think about it. I mean, come on. Peter will be okay. What's the worst thing that could happen?"

Later in the lunchroom, I sat at a table against the back wall, staring at my tray. Why did I take all this food? I wondered. My stomach feels as if it were made of lead. I can't eat a thing.

I heard a chair scrape against the floor. I looked up as Zack dropped down across from me. He ripped apart his brown paper lunch bag and unwrapped a sandwich. "Want to trade?" He poked the sandwich in my face. "It's tuna fish."

"No thanks," I murmured.

"Mom knows I hate tuna fish. So she packs a tuna fish sandwich every day."

"Help yourself to mine," I said, shoving the tray across the table. "I'm not hungry."

"What happened to you in Chem class?" he asked, grabbing the pizza slice off my tray. "You totally messed up."

I shrugged. "Yeah. I guess. I just . . . I couldn't remember the assignment. I studied it. It just all went out of my head."

The truth was, I barely heard a word anyone said to me all morning. All I could think about was my poor brother. Was he okay? What was I going to tell my parents when they returned home tonight?

I suddenly realized Zack had been talking. He was gazing at me, waiting for a reply.

"What?" I asked. "I'm sorry. I—"

"After school," he said. "I'm an ace in chemistry. You know. We could go over the chapters for the test."

"Uh . . . I'd like that, Zack. But I'd better not. My parents are still away. I have to take care of Peter."

Zack pushed his lips out in an exaggerated pout. "Peter can amuse himself while we study."

I felt terrible. Zack was being so nice. I was beginning to think he really liked me. But I couldn't spend time with him while Peter was still so messed up.

And I couldn't explain to Zack what I had done to my brother.

"I—I can't," I said. "Maybe tomorrow we can—"

"Yeah. Maybe," Zack grumbled. He stuffed the rest of my pizza into his mouth. "Do you want those pretzels?"

The afternoon dragged by. I couldn't concentrate. Couldn't think. I kept picturing Peter on his own at school, sitting in class in a total trance, unable to remember anything.

Maybe he made it through the day okay, I kept telling myself. Maybe he snapped out of it. When I meet him at his school, he'll be his jolly old self again.

It's possible, isn't it?

I couldn't wait to find out. I cut my last class. It was only gym, so it was no big deal. I waved to Addie on my way out of the high school, signaling that I'd call her later. Then I made my way to Peter's school, two blocks away.

It had rained hard during the day. Water had puddled along the curbs and street corners. A gusty breeze sent water dripping down from the swaying trees. The storm clouds were finally parting, allowing narrow beams of sunlight to filter down.

I jogged all the way to the elementary school, my shoes splashing up rainwater. The cool, moist air felt soothing on my hot cheeks.

I reached the school at exactly three o'clock, in time to hear the clang of the final bell. Inside the building I heard cheers, the scrape of chairs, slamming locker doors. A few seconds later, kids came streaming out of their classes.

I waited at the bottom of the front stairs. Crossing my arms in front of me, I kept my eyes on the double doors, eager for my brother to appear.

The doors banged open, and kids came charging out. Laughing, shouting, shoving each other, they swarmed around me as they made their way to the street.

Maybe Peter will be laughing and shouting too, I told myself. The way he always has in the past.

When Peter didn't appear in the first stampede of kids, I felt my neck muscles tense. Where was he?

I knew that Mrs. Andersen's class was second from the door. Peter was always one of the first ones out of the building.

Relax, Danielle! I scolded myself. It's not even ten after three yet. Don't hit the panic button too soon.

Car doors slammed. Bike chains clattered as kids pulled them free of the bike racks. A bright silver Frisbee whirred past my head.

The school doors banged open again, and a group of girls in Scout uniforms stepped out. They were followed by several little kids, being led by parents or nannies.

I checked my watch. Three-fifteen.

"Okay, Peter," I muttered. "Let's get going."

What was he doing in there? Probably hanging out with friends, forgetting all about me.

The laughter and shouts had faded. Most of the cars and school buses had pulled away with kids inside. A few more kids straggled out. Two boys hopped down the stairs, tossing a small plastic football back and forth.

"Hey—!" I called out. One of them looked a lot like Peter. But it wasn't.

I let out a long sigh and checked my watch again. Three twenty-three.

"Come on, Peter. Give me a break!" I groaned.

I couldn't help it. Fear started to tighten my throat. My stomach suddenly felt like lead again.

Where *is* he? I *told* him to meet me on these steps.

Very quiet now. The doors were closed. One last kid came wandering out, holding a Game Boy up in front of his face. He was concentrating so hard on the game, he tripped and fell down the stairs.

"Peter . . . Peter . . . " I repeated his name under my breath.

I didn't know whether to feel frightened or angry. I decided I had no choice. I couldn't stand out here all afternoon. I had to go in and get him.

My legs trembled as I climbed the stairs.

Stay calm, Danielle, I scolded myself again as I pulled open the door. He's either goofing with his friends. Or else he's talking with Mrs. Andersen, probably showing off, trying to impress her.

Mrs. Andersen was Peter's favorite teacher ever. He never stopped mentioning her. It was always "Mrs. Andersen said this," and "Mrs. Andersen said that." I think Mom has actually been getting a little jealous that Peter is so crazy about Mrs. Andersen.

The long front hall was empty. My shoes made a hollow sound as I walked toward Peter's classroom.

It's always strange going back to your old school. When I went here, the place seemed enormous. But now, the classrooms all appeared so tiny, the desks and tables so low to the ground. The water fountain was practically down at my knees!

I turned the first corner, and Mrs. Andersen's room came into view. I stepped up to the door, my heart pounding a little harder, and poked my head in. "Peter—?" No.

I uttered a disappointed sigh.

Mrs. Andersen sat at her desk, her head bowed, writing rapidly on a stack of papers. She looked up as I stepped into the room and narrowed her eyes at me. "Yes?"

She was a young woman with wavy blond hair, round, blue eyes, and a nice smile. She wore a pale blue sweater-vest over a white top. As I came closer, I could see why Peter liked her so much. She was really awesome looking!

She kept her pen poised over the papers as she watched me approach.

"I'm Danielle Warner," I said.

She didn't appear to recognize the name. "Can I help you, Danielle?" she asked. She had a soft, little-girl voice. She sounded more like a kid than a teacher.

"I was hoping to find my brother, Peter, in here," I said.

Her smile faded. "Peter?"

I nodded. "But I guess he already left. Did you see him leave? Was he with some of his friends?"

Mrs. Andersen lowered the pen to the desk. She squinted at me. "What is your brother's name? Did you say Peter?"

"Yes. Peter Warner. He was supposed to meet me out front. I've been waiting since the bell rang and—"

"Well, I think you have the wrong classroom," she interrupted.

I stared at her. "Excuse me? You're Mrs. Andersen, right?"

"Yes, I am," she said softly.

"Then this is the right room," I replied. "You're Peter's favorite teacher. He doesn't stop talking about you."

She stood up. Her expression became stern. "I'm really sorry, Danielle. But you've made a mistake. *I don't have anyone named Peter Warner in my class.*"

My mouth dropped open. I stared at her. "You're kidding, right? You are Peter's favorite teacher. You know Peter, right?"

She bit her bottom lip and shook her head. "No. I'm sorry. I—"

"Red hair!" I shouted. "Bright red eyeglasses. Never stops talking. You know. Peter!"

"Danielle," she said softly. "Why are you shouting at me? Your brother is not in my class. Maybe you mean Mr. *Anders*. Sometimes people get us mixed up since our names are so similar."

"No!" I cried. "I'm not mixed-up. Peter is in your class, Mrs. Andersen. I *know* he is."

She sighed and raised her eyes to the door, as if searching for help. "You need to try the office," she said softly. "Mrs. Beck can help you find Peter. She'll know whose class he's in."

I stared at her, breathing hard. I had my hands

pressed against my waist. My brain was spinning. Mrs. Andersen . . . Mrs. Andersen . . . Peter talked about her constantly.

No way I had the name wrong.

"Mrs. Beck," she repeated. She motioned to the door. "You'd better hurry if you want to catch her. She leaves early on Mondays."

"Oh . . . okay," I said softly. I turned and made my way out of the classroom. The little desks . . . the chalkboards so low on the wall . . . the water fountain nearly down on the floor . . . it all suddenly appeared unreal. As if I were back in another nightmare.

I made my way toward the front office. My shoes thudded loudly, echoing in the empty hall. Two teachers walked by, laughing softly about something.

I stopped at the office. The door was closed. The lights were off.

"Mrs. Beck already left," one of the teachers called to me. They disappeared around a corner.

I stared through the glass into the dark office. "Peter, where are you?" I murmured.

I walked through the halls, making a complete circle of the building. I looked into every classroom I passed. No sign of my brother.

Did he go home without me? I wondered.

Did he forget he was supposed to meet me? Did he go out a side door and walk home by himself?

Yes. That had to be the answer. Just thinking it made me feel a lot better.

I hurried outside and practically leaped down the front steps. I ran all the way home.

He's already home. I know it. The little creep is already home.

I burst into the house and heaved my backpack to the floor. "Peter, are you here?" I called breathlessly.

No reply.

I raced down the hall toward the kitchen. "Peter? Are you home?"

No sign of him in the kitchen. I checked the den. The dining room. "Peter? Hey, Peter?"

I stopped and listened.

Silence.

Then I heard a sound that sent a shiver down my back.

A moan. A low moan. Like an animal in pain.

"Peter? Is that you?" I followed the sound to the front stairs. I grabbed the banister.

Another moan, followed by a high-pitched howl.

Gripping the railing tightly, I pulled myself up the stairs. "Peter? Is that you? I'm coming."

I reached the top, my heart thudding, and hurried down the hall to his room. The door stood open. I dove into the doorway—and gasped. "Peter?"

He was pacing back and forth in the middle of the

room. He still had his jacket on. His eyes were nearly shut.

"Peter—?"

He had his hands shoved deep in his jeans pockets. He kept moaning to himself, moaning like a sick animal, shaking his head as he paced.

Why were his eyes closed like that? Why was he making those horrible sounds? What was he doing?"

"Peter, stop!" I cried. "Stop! Can you hear me? What are you doing?"

He moaned again, his eyes still nearly shut.

I could feel my throat tighten in fear. "You were supposed to meet me," I said. "Will you stop doing that? What is *wrong* with you?"

Finally, he stopped pacing. He turned toward me. His eyes opened slowly. He studied me for a long moment, his face filled with confusion.

When he finally spoke, his words came out in a hoarse growl: "Who are you? What are you doing in my house?"

I gasped. A wave of nausea rolled up, tightening my throat. I suddenly felt so sick, I clapped a hand over my mouth to keep from hurling.

"Peter, don't you remember me? *Don't* you?"

He narrowed his eyes at me. "Get out of my house."

"I'm your sister!" I cried.

Poor Peter. I had to do something.

"Peter, just stay here in your room," I said. "You'll be okay. I promise."

He stared blankly at me through his glasses. I could tell that he had no idea who I was.

I spun away and ran down the hall. My mind was racing. What could I do? Who should I call?

I ran into my parents' room and frantically ran-sacked their desk drawers until I found their phone book. My hands were shaking so badly, I could barely turn the pages.

My stomach was lurching again. I found Dr. Ross's

number and quickly punched it into the phone.

It rang three times before a woman answered. "Doctor's office."

"I've got to speak to Dr. Ross," I said breathlessly. "It—it's an emergency."

"I'm sorry," she replied. "He's away at a conference this week. If you'd like to leave a message, I could—"

"No thanks!" I cried. I clicked off the phone.

Who else? Who else?

Aunt Kate. She lives in the next town. Aunt Kate is a sensible, practical woman. She's always calm. She always knows what to do.

I punched in her number. "Please be there," I murmured. "Please . . ."

The phone rang and rang. I let it ring at least ten or twelve times before I finally gave up.

"Now what?"

Who can I call? There's *got* to be someone!

I shut my eyes and tried to think. A loud knock on the front door made me jump.

"Who is that? Addie?"

The knocking repeated, louder this time.

I tossed down the phone and made my way quickly down the stairs to the front door.

Maybe Addie can think of someone who will help me, I told myself.

I pulled the door open.

Not Addie.

I stared in terror at the man in the black raincoat.

"Wh-what do you want?" I asked.

"Gotcha," he whispered.

He lowered his head toward me like a bird about to attack a worm. He had a short black beard and mustache, and wavy black hair that fell over his forehead. He glared at me with round, black eyes.

His gaze was so cold, I felt a chill run down my back. Then he raised his eyes to look behind me into the house. "Are your parents here?" His voice was soft and scratchy, as if he had a sore throat.

"No," I said.

Why did I say that? How stupid! Why did I tell him my parents weren't home?

"I mean, they'll be home really soon. Sorry. I have to go." My heart pounding, I moved to close the door.

But he pushed past me, nearly bumping me aside.

He was in the house!

He stood in the entryway, still glaring at me with those tiny black eyes. "You ran from me this morning. . . ."

"Y-yes," I replied. "I didn't know—I mean . . . who are you? What do you want?"

"Sorry if I frightened you," he said in that scratchy voice. "I'm a reporter. For the *Star-Journal*."

"Huh? A reporter?"

I suddenly felt very foolish.

A newspaper reporter? But why had he been chasing me? And why had he been spying on our house?

He's lying, I thought. Why did I open the door without looking first? Why did I let him in the house? Why was I so stupid?

He glimpsed himself in the hall mirror and pushed back his wavy black hair with one hand. "I'm thinking of doing a story about your house," he said.

I studied him, trying to figure out if this was some kind of joke. "Are you selling something?" I asked. "Insurance or something? Because if that's what you're trying to do—"

He raised his right hand. "No. I'm a reporter. Really." He fumbled in his back pocket and pulled out a worn brown wallet. He flipped it open to show me a card that had his photo on it and said PRESS at the top.

"I found some old articles at the newspaper office. A big stack of yellowed papers hidden away in a corner cabinet. In the old articles, they call this house *Forget-Me House*." His eyes burned into mine.

I stared hard at him. "Huh? Why?"

He shrugged. "I'm not sure. According to the papers I found, the house makes people forget."

My heart started to pound. "Forget what?"

"Forget themselves," he replied. "One by one, one at a time, the people who live here forget everything. And then . . . then . . . they are forgotten too. Forgotten forever."

I wanted to scream, but I held it in. I pictured Peter up in his room. Peter didn't remember me. He couldn't remember his own sister.

The reporter leaned closer, narrowing his cold eyes at me. "Has anything strange happened to you?"

My breath caught in my throat. "N-no," I choked out. I didn't want to tell him.

I had to think. Had to figure this out.

He studied me. "Are you sure? Have you seen anything strange? Heard anything? Is anyone in your family acting weird?"

"No!" I cried. "No! Please—you have to leave!"

"I'm sorry. I didn't mean to scare you," the reporter said. "It's just a bunch of old newspaper stories. Probably not true."

He stepped back, shifting his black raincoat on his shoulders. "I see I've upset you. I'll come back. I'll come back when your parents are home."

I heard a noise and turned to the stairs. "Peter— is that you?"

Silence.

When I turned back, the reporter was gone.

I stood staring out at the street, trying to stop my

head from spinning. My mind whirred with questions.

Was he telling the truth? Did those old articles explain what was happening to Peter?

Was it possible that I never hypnotized my brother? That Peter's strange behavior wasn't my fault at all? That it was all the house's fault?

Forget-Me House . . .

I remembered Peter's desperate plea. *"Danielle, don't forget me. Please—don't forget me!"*

"One by one, the people who live here forget everything."

The reporter's words repeated in my ears.

"They forget everything. Then they are forgotten too."

"But that's *crazy!*" I muttered. "Crazy." I realized my whole body was shaking. I turned back into the house and closed the front door behind me.

To my surprise, Peter stood right behind me.

"Get *out!*" he screamed. His eyes were wild. His red hair stood straight up. His body was tensed, as if ready to attack. "Get out! Get out of my house!"

I didn't have time to reply.

He leaped at me—and wrapped his hands around my throat.

"Get out! Get out!"

"Peter, no!" I shrieked. His hands tightened, cutting off my words.

"Peter, stop! You're choking me! I . . . can't . . . breathe. . . ."

He opened his mouth in an animal growl. His fingers tightened around my throat.

I dropped to my knees, struggling to free myself. I wheezed as I struggled to take in air.

I grabbed his arms and tried to pull his hands off me. But he was suddenly so strong, so strong.

"Can't breathe!" I gasped. "Please!"

I staggered to my feet. Frantically grabbed him around the waist. And falling forward, stumbling, choking, I slammed him into the wall.

His hands slid off me. He uttered a startled cry.

I shoved him out of the way and burst out the front door. Sucking in breath after breath, I jumped off the front stoop and kept running. Down the front lawn, leaping over a coiled garden hose my dad had left there. Over the sidewalk, onto the street.

I ran. Not thinking. Not feeling anything. My throat aching, throbbing.

Peter . . . Peter . . . Peter . . .

His name repeated in my mind like some kind of

terrifying chant. I couldn't stop it. I heard his name each time my shoes thudded on the pavement.

Peter . . . Peter . . . Peter . . .

My brother had become a wild animal. A wild animal in a rage.

Why was he suddenly so angry? Was it because of what the reporter had told me? Because he was forgetting everything? Losing himself?

Was Peter in a total rage because of what the house was doing to him?

I ran through an intersection without stopping, without seeing anything. I heard a car horn honk. I heard an angry shout.

"Danielle, you've got to think clearly," I scolded myself. But how *could* I think clearly? My own brother didn't remember me. And now he had nearly strangled me.

I kept running.

I can't go home, I told myself. It isn't safe. It isn't safe with Peter there.

But I *have* to go back! I argued with myself. I'm in charge. I'm responsible for Peter. I can't just leave him there all alone, prowling around like a lost animal.

It was nearly dinnertime. My parents were on their way home. They would be back in an hour or two.

And then what?

How could I explain to them what had happened?

Would they blame me for Peter? Would they believe me about the reporter's story? Could they *do* anything to save my poor brother?

Without realizing it, I had run to Addie's house. I rang the bell and pounded on the door at the same time. "Addie, are you home? Addie—?" I called in a high, shrill voice.

After a few seconds, the door swung open. Addie gaped at me. "Danielle? What's wrong? You look horrible!"

"I—I—" I couldn't talk. I stumbled past her, into the front room. The TV was on. A local newscast.

Am I going to be on the news too? I suddenly wondered. Talking about how my poor brother went crazy because we live in *Forget-Me House*?

"Danielle—?" Addie placed a hand on my trembling shoulder. "What is it? It's cold out. You don't have a jacket or anything?"

I shook my head, still struggling to catch my breath. "I just ran," I finally choked out. "I had to run. Peter!"

Addie narrowed her green eyes. "Peter?"

"Yeah," I rushed on. "I don't think he was ever hypnotized. I think it's something else. Something much more scary."

"Oh. Right. Peter!" Addie stared at me. "Is he still acting weird?"

I nodded. "He—he tried to choke me."

She gasped. "Where are your parents? They're not back yet?"

I glanced at the clock above the TV. Nearly six. "Soon," I said. "They should be home soon."

"Do you want to wait here until they get back?" Addie asked.

I sighed. "I guess." I dropped onto her couch. I shut my eyes and buried my head in my hands.

And saw them. The eerie, slime-covered kids in the basement. I saw their sad faces. Heard them chanting my brother's name. And suddenly I knew. I knew who they were.

They were the forgotten ones.

They were the victims of *Forget-Me House*.

And now the forgotten kids were calling for Peter.

I jumped to my feet and let out a shrill scream. "Nooooo!" And without even realizing it, I was running again. Out the door and down Addie's front yard.

I heard Addie calling to me. But I didn't stop or look back.

Once again I ran without seeing, my mind a blur. I ran the whole way home.

What would I find there?

Would my brother try to attack me again? Would he still be a wild, raging animal?

I fought back my fear. I knew I had no choice. I had to be there. I had to save Peter. I had to be home when Mom and Dad returned. To warn them. To explain to them.

As I turned the corner onto our block, I heard a sharp animal cry. A dog bark. Without slowing down, I turned and saw our neighbor's large gray German shepherd racing after me.

"No, boy! Go home! Go home!" I pleaded. Why was he acting like this?

And what was his name?

Why couldn't I remember his name?

Running hard, the big dog barked a warning, its tail wagging furiously. It caught up to me easily. And then it jumped in front of me.

I stumbled over it.

It leaped up, panting hard, pushing its paws against my waist.

I screamed at him, "Go home! Please—down! Get down!"

Then I realized the dog only wanted to play.

"Not now. Please—not now." I grabbed its front paws and lowered them to the pavement. I petted the dog's head.

Why couldn't I remember its name?

"Not now, boy. Go home!"

I started running again, the dog yapping at my heels. I had the sudden hope that my parents' car would be in the driveway. Please, I thought, be there. Be home to help me. Maybe the three of us working together can do something to help Peter.

But . . . no car. The driveway stood empty. The front door to the house was wide-open, just as I'd left it when I ran from Peter.

My heart pounding, I started up the front lawn. And realized the dog was no longer at my feet. I turned and saw it at the curb. It gazed up at the house, uttering low, whimpering sounds. Its ears were down, tail between its legs, its whole body hunched, trembling.

It's terrified, I realized. The dog won't come up here. It's terrified.

Finally the dog lowered its gaze. It shook itself hard, and still whimpering, slinked away.

I had the sudden impulse to follow it. To run away. To find a place that was safe, a place that didn't make dogs tremble and cry.

But my brother was inside the house. And he was in trouble.

I had no choice.

I took a deep breath and went inside.

And as soon as I entered, I saw the basement door. Wide-open.

And I heard the whispered voices, harsh and raspy. The voices rising up from the basement.

But this time they weren't chanting my brother's name.

This time they were chanting my name, over and over.

"Danielle . . . Danielle . . . Danielle . . ."

I pressed my hands against my cheeks—and cried out in horror.

My face—it felt wet. Wet and sticky.

Frantically I clawed at the goo, tearing at it, pulling it, rubbing it off my face.

And all the while, the voices droned on: "*Danielle . . . Danielle . . . Danielle . . .*"

"Noooo!" A cry of terror escaped my throat as I pulled the last of the slime away. "You're not going to get me. You're not going to get Peter."

Somehow I had to save Peter—if I wasn't already too late!

"Peter?" I choked out. My voice sounded tiny and hollow. I grabbed the banister and called up the front stairs. "Peter? Are you in your room?"

No reply.

I ran upstairs. Checked his room. Then mine. No sign of him.

"Peter?"

I hurried downstairs. I had no choice. A wave of cold dread swept over me as I approached the basement door.

The chanting had stopped. Silence now. A deep silence that rang in my ears.

It took all my strength to step into the stairwell and peer down to the basement. "Peter?"

I knew he was down there.

I knew I had to go down and bring him back upstairs.

"Peter, this is your sister. Danielle," I called down. "I know you don't remember me. But this is Danielle. I'm coming down now. I'm coming to help you."

I listened hard. No reply.

Then I heard a creaking sound. Very slow. A low grinding. Like a heavy door opening.

"Peter? Did you hear me? This is your sister. I'm coming down to help you."

I took a deep, shuddering breath. I spotted the long metal flashlight on the top step. I picked it up. A good weapon. I hoped I wouldn't need to use it.

"Peter, here I come."

My legs were shaking so badly, I had to take the stairs one at a time. I stopped every few steps and listened. Wind rattled the windowpanes at ground level. The only sound except for my shallow breaths.

Halfway down the stairs, I heard another creak. Then a soft, scraping sound. "Peter? Is that you? Can you hear me?"

No reply.

I forced myself down the rest of the way. Gripping the flashlight tightly in my right hand, I spun away from the stairs and gazed into the basement.

In the darkening evening light from the narrow windows above, I could see the clutter of junk, old furniture, stacks of old newspapers.

"Oh." My mouth dropped open as I turned to the far wall, the wall across from the enormous, time-blackened furnace, and saw the scrawled words.

Words at least a foot tall, scrawled in red paint. Still wet, dripping over the jagged, cracked stones.

DON'T FORGET ME.

Still wet. Just painted. Dark red paint. Red as blood.

DON'T FORGET ME.

And before I got over the shock of seeing that—I saw Peter.

I blinked once. Twice. Not quite believing.

Yes. Peter. In a doorway to a smaller room beyond the furnace.

Peter, bathed in a strange, silvery light. His back to me. His hair still on end. His shirt untucked over baggy jeans. Peter, not moving. Caught in the eerie light, standing so still in the tiny back room.

I opened my mouth to call to him. But no sound came out.

My cold, wet hand slid over the metal flashlight. I gripped it tighter. And took a trembling step toward him. And then another.

Stepping around the clutter of junk in the center of the room. The painted words, the dripping, blood-red words still in view at my side.

DON'T FORGET ME.

"Peter? Can you hear me?"

He didn't answer. Didn't move.

"I'm coming to help you. I am your sister. Danielle. Do you remember me? Do you?"

I stopped just outside the low doorway to the back room. And realized that Peter was leaning down into another opening. A dark opening. At first, I thought it was some kind of hole in the basement wall.

But as I blinked it into focus, I realized that Peter was standing in front of a tall trapdoor. A door that had raised up from the basement floor.

A door that led—where?

Leaning into the black opening, he took a step down.

"Nooooo!" I screeched. "Stop! Listen to me! Turn around! Peter, turn around!"

He froze. He didn't move.

I screamed again. I begged him to turn around.

And then, slowly . . . so slowly . . . he took a step back from the dark opening. He took a step back and then . . . slowly . . . bathed in the eerie light, turned to face me.

And as he turned, I uttered a sick cry. My stomach heaved. My knees buckled.

And I stared at him in horror.

Stared at the thick layer of mucus over his face. The clear gelatin that covered his hair, his face, his eyes!

His mouth!

The thick layer of goo glistened wetly under the silvery light.

And as I gaped in horror, unable to speak, unable to move, Peter opened his mouth. The gelatin bubbled over his mouth.

And I heard his muffled word!

"Good-bye."

"Stop!" I screamed. "Where are you going? What are you doing?"

But he didn't seem to hear me.

The thick jelly bubbled over his mouth. His eyes stared out from behind the shimmering layer of goo.

Then he turned and stepped into the darkness.

"Stop! No—stop!" I pleaded. I took off, racing to him, my shoes sliding on the dusty, concrete floor.

He lowered himself into a black pit beyond the trapdoor.

As I ran, I reached out to him, stretched out my arms to grab him and pull him back.

But the trapdoor snapped shut with a thundering *bang*.

Dust flew up all around me.

I covered my eyes, waiting for it to settle. I could taste it in my mouth, feel it in my lungs.

Then, forcing my eyes open, I dropped to my knees. I reached for the door to pry it up. To open it and free my brother.

But the basement floor was solid and smooth. I couldn't see the door. I couldn't see any trace of a door.

Frantically I slid my hands over the floor, searching . . . searching.

"Peter, where are you? Where did you go?"

No door. No door. Not the tiniest crack in the floor. I uttered an angry cry. I slapped the floor with both fists, sending up another cloud of dust.

"Don't worry, Peter. I'll get you out of there," I said, struggling to my feet.

As I ran to the stairs, I rubbed the thick dust from my hands onto my jeans. The floor seemed to tilt and sway beneath me. The walls spun wildly.

My brain whirring, I hurtled forward. Pulled myself up the groaning basement stairs. Into the kitchen.

I grabbed the phone off the wall.

I'll call the police. I'll call the fire department. They can open the trapdoor. They can get Peter out of there.

I raised my hand to dial 911. But I stopped as yellow light swept over the kitchen from outside.

Twin beams of yellow light. Headlights.

I heard the crunch of tires over gravel.

"Yes!" I ran to the back window. "Yes!"

Mom and Dad were home. "Yes!"

I tore open the kitchen door and ran out, screaming, waving both hands above my head wildly.

I leaped in front of the car. Into the wide rectangle of yellow light. "Mom! Dad! You've got to hurry! Help! You've got to help!"

I grabbed Mom's car door and tugged it open. "Hurry! Get out! There's no time!" I shrieked.

I saw their startled faces. I grabbed Mom's arm and started to pull her out of the car. But her seat belt was still attached. She let out a cry of protest.

The driver's door swung open, and Dad climbed out, frowning at me, his eyes darting from me to the house. "What's wrong? Danielle, what is it?" he cried.

"No time!" I wailed. "No time to explain! Hurry!"

Mom finally unsnapped her seat belt. She slid out of the car and stood unsteadily in front of me. "What's all the screaming? Is—is something wrong in the house?"

I grabbed her hand and tugged her toward the kitchen door. "It's Peter!" I cried. "He—he's in the basement. I mean—"

"Peter?" Dad squinted at me.

"Please! We have to hurry!" I shrieked. "Peter went down a trapdoor. It's a long story—but he's been acting so strange. Ever since you left! Come on! We have to go down there! Why are you just *standing* there?"

They stood side by side now, both staring hard at me.

"Danielle, *who* is in the basement?" Mom asked finally.

"Peter!" I screamed frantically.

"But *who* is Peter?" Dad asked.

"Huh?" My mouth dropped open. "Peter! My brother! What is *wrong* with you two? Hurry! We've got to get him out!"

They didn't move. Just stood there staring with such worried expressions on their faces.

Finally Dad came over and put his hands gently on my shoulders. "Danielle, please—calm down," he said. "What is this all about?"

"You know you don't have a brother," Mom said softly. "You know there's no one in our family named Peter."

"Have you gone crazy?" I shrieked. "Of course I have a brother! Have you both gone totally crazy?"

Dad tightened his hold on my shoulders. "Danielle, please," he whispered. "Let's go in the house and talk about this quietly."

Mom sighed. "Your father and I have had a very long trip."

"But, Peter—!" I protested. "He's in the basement. We can't just leave him there."

Mom sighed again. "I knew we shouldn't have left her alone," she said to Dad.

Dad kept his eyes locked on mine. He shook his head. "Danielle, you used to make up imaginary friends when you were little. But you're fifteen now."

I pulled free from his grip. "I'm *not* making Peter up!" I cried. "I'm not! He's my brother! He's your *son!*"

Mom shut her eyes and held her hands over her

ears. "Please stop it. Please. I have a splitting head-ache."

"Can't we go inside and talk about this calmly?" Dad pleaded. "We'll sit down and have a cup of tea, and—"

"*How can I be calm?*" I wailed. "Peter is in horrible trouble—and you don't even remember him! Your own son! Your own son!"

I grabbed Dad's hands and pulled him toward the house. "Come down to the basement. I'll show you."

Walking with me, Dad slipped his arm around my shoulder. "It'll be okay, Danielle," he said softly. I saw him glance at Mom. "You can show us the basement later. Okay?"

He pressed his palm against my forehead. "Hmmm. It feels hot. I think you might have a fever. That would explain—"

"NO!" I shrieked. "I'm not sick! And I'm not crazy! You've *got* to remember Peter. You've got to!"

They led me into the house. They took me up to my room and forced a thermometer into my mouth. I didn't have any fever.

But they insisted I get into bed. Dad went downstairs to call Dr. Ross.

Mom kept clearing her throat tensely, crossing and uncrossing her arms, sighing loudly. All the while, she gaped at me as if I was some kind of alien from another planet.

I changed into my pajamas and sat on the edge of my bed. "I know what's happening here," I told her. "Peter is real. But you've forgotten him. Because this is *Forget-Me House*."

Mom narrowed her eyes at me. "Excuse me? This is *what?*"

"*Forget-Me House*," I repeated. "A man came here. He told me—"

"Someone was here?" Mom interrupted.

I nodded. "And he told me this would happen."

Mom sighed for the hundredth time. "I don't understand. A strange man came here? And he said you would start to imagine you had a brother?"

"I'm not imagining!" I cried. And then I totally lost it. I jumped to my feet. I grabbed Mom by the shoulders, and I started to shake her. "Listen to me! Listen to me! You've got to listen to me!"

Mom's eyes bulged in shock, in fear. "Danielle, stop! Let go!" she pleaded.

I heard footsteps. Dad rushed into the room. He uttered a startled cry. Then he pulled me off Mom. He wrapped his arm around my waist and guided me firmly back to my bed.

"Sit down, Danielle," he ordered. "Sit down and take a deep breath. Do I have to take you to the hospital?"

"She—she *attacked* me!" Mom whimpered, rubbing her shoulders. And then she added, "Like a wild animal."

"Dr. Ross will see us tomorrow," Dad told me. He stood between Mom and me, breathing hard, hands on his waist. He stood tensed, as if ready to protect Mom from another attack.

"She's completely out of control," Mom said, shaking her head. The tears in her eyes began to run down her cheeks.

"I—I'm sorry," I told her. "I didn't mean to hurt you. I only . . . " My voice trailed off.

They're not going to listen to me, I realized. They're not going to believe me.

They think I've gone crazy or something.

They really don't remember Peter.

What can I do?

I've got to wait, I decided. I've got to wait until everyone is calmer. Then I can sit down quietly with them and explain. Explain about the house. Explain what that reporter told me about this place.

I hunched myself on the edge of the bed, hands clasped tightly in my lap. My hair fell over my face, but I made no attempt to push it back.

"Sorry, Mom," I repeated. "Sorry I've been acting so insane. But we really need to talk. About Peter and about this house."

Mom and Dad exchanged glances.

"Of course, we'll talk," Dad said, sounding really forced and phony. "We'll talk about everything. You know, moving into a new house can be very, very stressful."

I wanted to argue with him, but I bit my tongue.

Mom wiped the tears off her cheeks. She suddenly appeared so tired, so old. "Let's discuss the whole thing in the morning," she said. She pressed her fingers against her temples. "When we're all calm and rested, and I don't have this splitting headache."

"Okay," I agreed.

"Yes, first thing in the morning," Dad added, nodding eagerly. "I know you'll feel a lot better about everything after a good night's sleep."

No, I won't! That's what I wanted to say. Instead, I murmured, "Yeah. Okay."

Mom started toward the door, then turned back to me. She forced a smile to her face. "Tell you what," she said. "I'll make your favorite—blueberry pancakes—for breakfast. How does that sound?"

"Great," I replied.

"Okay!" Dad said cheerfully. "Blueberry pancakes for breakfast. And we'll have a nice, long talk."

Dad put a hand on Mom's shoulder, and they hurried out of the room. They both seemed really eager to get away.

I know they're going to go downstairs and talk about me, I thought. About how crazy I am and how I totally lost it.

I'll set them straight in the morning, I decided. I'll take them down to the basement. I'll convince them that Peter is real. And together, we'll rescue my poor brother—from wherever he is.

I yawned loudly. All the tension, all the worry, all the *horror*—it made me feel so tired, so exhausted. I suddenly felt as if I weighed a thousand pounds. I couldn't raise my arms. I couldn't keep my eyes open.

"First thing in the morning!" I murmured to myself. "First thing . . . "

I fell into a deep, dreamless sleep.

Bright morning sunlight through my window startled me awake. I blinked hard, feeling dazed. Such a deep sleep. I groaned as I sat up. I didn't feel at all rested.

What kept me awake? I wondered. What was troubling me?

I gazed around the room, squinting against the bright light.

Something had upset me yesterday. But what? What *was* it? What had me so worried?

I couldn't remember.

I lowered my feet to the floor and climbed out of bed. I was still thinking hard, still trying to remember what had kept me awake for most of the night.

"Peter," I whispered finally. The word floated out as if from a distant place. "Peter."

Yes. Peter. Of course. Peter.

"Oh, no," I murmured. "Oh, no. Oh, no . . ." I had nearly forgotten him.

Peter was almost lost. Almost lost forever. And then I realized . . .

"I'm next."

"Peter . . . Peter . . ." Chanting his name so I wouldn't forget it, I hurried into the bathroom to shower. Then I pulled on an oversized blue sweater over black leggings.

As I made my way downstairs, I rehearsed what I was going to say to my parents. First I'd explain how strange Peter had been acting. How at first I thought it was because I hypnotized him.

Then I'd tell them about the reporter who came to

the door. And what he told me about the strange, frightening rumors about this house. I'd tell them why the house is known as *Forget-Me House.*

I'll be totally calm, I decided. I'll speak slowly and softly. They'll see that I'm not crazy. They'll believe me.

"Calm . . . calm . . ." I repeated to myself as I made my way down the back hall to the kitchen. But my heart started to pound. And my hands suddenly felt ice-cold.

"Calm . . . calm . . ."

I stepped into the kitchen.

And gasped in shock.

"Mom? Dad?"

I uttered a hoarse cry as I gazed around the dark, empty kitchen.

"Hey! Where are you?"

I clicked on the ceiling lights. My heart racing, I walked around the kitchen.

No sign of them. No breakfast dishes on the table or on the sink. No coffee cups. No cereal bowls.

"Mom? Dad? Did you leave?" I tried to shout, but my voice came out tiny and weak.

"That's impossible," I muttered to myself.

I hurried to the kitchen window and peered out. No car in the driveway.

Did they go to work? Did they just drive off?

They must have left a note, I decided. They always leave me endless notes on the refrigerator. I turned. Bumped my knee on a kitchen stool.

"Ouch!" I hopped across the kitchen on one foot.

No. No note stuck to the fridge.

"Weird."

Rubbing my throbbing knee, I hurried upstairs to their bedroom. "Hey, are you two still asleep?"

I stepped into the room. Mom's nightgown lay crumpled on the floor beside their unmade bed. The suitcases from their trip had been emptied and stood open against the far wall. The light in their bathroom had been left on.

"Where *are* you?" How could they leave for work without even waking me up? And what about the blueberry pancakes? What about our serious talk?

What about Peter?

"They promised. . . ." I murmured as I headed back to my room to get ready for school. I suddenly felt so angry. And so hurt. "They promised. . . ."

The morning went by in a slow-motion blur. What did my teachers talk about? Did any of my friends talk to me? I couldn't tell you.

I shouldn't have come to school today, I told myself as I trudged like a zombie, a brain-dead zombie, from class to class. I should have stayed home. Called my parents. Called the police. Called *somebody* to come help me rescue Peter.

"Peter, I haven't forgotten you," I whispered

sadly. "Don't worry. I haven't forgotten."

But I kept repeating his name over. And I wrote it twenty times in my notebook in bright-red ink. Just to make sure he didn't slip away again.

At noon, I made my way into the lunchroom. Such a blur of faces . . . trays . . . laughing, talking kids.

Such a blur . . . such a dark blur . . .

Dark . . . darker . . .

"Huh?" Someone was shaking me.

Someone was squeezing my shoulders, squeezing so hard it hurt. Shaking me. Shaking me.

I blinked open my eyes. I struggled to see. "Addie—?"

She gripped my shoulders. Her face was bright red. She was breathing hard. "Danielle . . . Danielle, I—I couldn't get you to wake up."

I squinted at her, feeling dizzy, the lunchroom spinning.

"I shook you and shook you. You wouldn't open your eyes. I was so scared."

She dropped into a chair across the table from me. Her face was drenched in sweat. "I was so worried," she said, shuddering. "You—you passed out or something."

"I'm fine," I whispered. I cleared my throat. "Really. I feel perfectly fine. I guess I just . . . dozed off for a minute."

She lowered her gaze to the tabletop. "You're

okay? Well . . . where's your lunch?"

"Huh?" I stared down at the table too. "Oh. Uh . . . I think I brought one. I . . . I don't remember where I put it."

She squinted at me. "You're sitting here with no lunch?"

I shrugged.

Addie tugged at a strand of her hair, twisting it around one finger. "Well, do you feel like eating? You can share my lunch." She shoved the brown paper bag across the table toward me.

"I'm . . . not too hungry," I said.

"Didn't you see me waving to you in the auditorium during that boring assembly this morning?" she asked. "Why didn't you come over?"

"I didn't see you," I said. "I—I'm not too together today, Addie."

She rolled her eyes. "As if I couldn't see that? What is your problem, Danielle? When Mrs. Melton asked you to pass out the test papers, you just stared at her as if you didn't understand English."

I blinked. "I did? Really? I don't remember."

Addie squeezed my hand. "You sure you feel okay?"

"I'm not okay," I confessed, my voice breaking with emotion. "I'm not okay. I'm so worried, Addie. About Peter. He-he disappeared in the basement. And when my parents got home, they wouldn't believe me. They said that—"

"Wait. Wait." Addie made a time-out sign. "*Who* disappeared? *Who* disappeared in the basement?"

"Peter," I said. "He went into a trapdoor, and it closed, and then—"

"Who?" Addie looked totally bewildered. "Danielle, who is Peter?"

What happened next?

Did I try to explain to Addie? Or did I jump up from the table and run out of the lunchroom?

Did I stay in school and go to classes that afternoon? Did I wander around the school grounds until the final bell rang? Did I bolt out of the building at lunchtime with Addie calling after me and run all the way home?

I don't know. My mind was a blank.

When Addie couldn't remember Peter, something inside me snapped. I guess my fear took over.

I don't remember what happened next. My memory vanished in a swirl of terrified thoughts and cold panic.

Somehow I found myself on the front stoop of our new house. The afternoon sun was lowering itself behind the trees. I saw a squirrel scampering across the gray tiles of our roof.

I tried the front door. Locked. I had forgotten to take my key.

Mom was probably home. She usually gets home in the middle of the afternoon. I tried the doorbell. I pressed it hard. Pressed it again. Then I remembered it wasn't hooked up.

So I raised my fist, and pounded on the solid wood door.

Please be home, I thought. *Please be home, Mom. We've got to save Peter. We've got to save him before everyone forgets!*

I pounded some more, harder. Until my fist ached.

Finally, the door swung open. My mother stuck her head out. She squinted at me. "Yes?" she asked. "Can I help you?"

"Huh? It's *me!*" I cried.

Mom squinted harder. "I'm sorry. What can I do for you, miss?"

"It's me! It's ME!" I shrieked. "I'm your daughter!" I grabbed the storm door and jerked it open all the way.

Mom gasped. Her face tightened with fear. "Daughter? I don't understand. What daughter—?"

"*Let me in!*" I screamed. "You *can't* forget me! You can't! And you can't forget Peter, either!"

I lowered my shoulder and shoved her hard, out of the way.

She cried out and stumbled back into the entryway.

I hurtled into the house. The storm door slammed behind me.

"Get out!" Mom screamed. "What do you want? Get out of my house!"

"No! You come with me!" I shouted breathlessly. I grabbed her around the waist and pushed her roughly into the back hall.

"Let go of me!" she wailed. She squirmed and

struggled. She grabbed my arms and tried to pry them off her. "Who are you? What do you want?"

My heart pounded so hard, my chest felt about to explode. "You're coming to the basement," I said through gritted teeth. I gave her another hard shove. "I'm going to prove to you—"

"Do you want money?" she demanded. "Is that it? You want money? Okay. I don't have much in the house. But I'll give you what I have. Just . . . don't hurt me. Please—don't hurt me."

She looked so terrified, I dropped my hands. I let her go. "Mom!"

She backed away, her eyes wide with fear. "Money?" she whispered. "Is that what you want? If I give you money, will you go?"

"I don't want money!" I screamed. "I want you to remember me! And Peter!"

"Okay, okay." She trembled in fear. "I remember you. Yes. I do. I remember you. Is that good?"

She's terrified of me, her own daughter, I realized.

I could feel tears welling in my eyes. But I knew I had no time to waste.

She's not going to believe me, I saw. She's not going to recognize me. She's too frightened to listen to me, to let me prove anything to her.

What can I do? What?

I spun away from her. And lurched down the hall to the basement door. "Peter—I'm coming!" I called down the stairs. I jumped into the stairwell and began racing down, taking the stairs two at a time. "Peter, I haven't forgotten you. I'm coming!"

I heard footsteps above my head. My mother running across the floor. And then I heard her on the phone, her voice trembling, shrill, so frightened. My own mother, desperately calling the police.

"Yes. A strange girl. She broke into the house. She's acting very crazy. I—I think she's dangerous. Yes. Send someone. Right away."

"I'm not a strange girl," I said out loud.

I wanted to run back upstairs and argue with her. *Plead* with her to believe me. *Beg* her to remember me.

But I heard a creaking sound. On the other side of the basement.

I turned away from the stairs and made my way toward the little room in back. Late afternoon sunlight slanted in from the basement windows, sending long, orange stripes across the cluttered floor.

"I'm coming, Peter," I called, my voice hollow, ringing off the stone walls. "I'm here."

At the entrance to the backroom, I stopped with a gasp.

The trapdoor—it was creaking open. Slowly. Stone grinding against stone.

I could see only blackness beneath it. A dark pit that appeared to stretch down forever.

Slowly, slowly, the door lifted. As it opened, the

blackness seemed to spread across the floor, over the room. Shutting out the sunlight, shutting out all light.

And then, out of the darkness, a thin, silvery figure appeared.

He seemed to form in front of my eyes, shimmering wetly against the opening trapdoor.

I cried out when I recognized my brother. He stood so stiffly, trapped inside the thick layer of mucus. His hair, his face, his entire body wrapped tightly in that wet, clear covering.

He staggered toward me stiffly, and then raised one arm, motioning to me. Behind the thick goo, I could see his glasses, and behind them, his eyes, staring out at me so blankly.

"Peter—!" I choked out.

He was almost colorless. Entirely gray. I could practically see through him.

He motioned with the one hand. And his mouth opened slightly. Opened, then closed, forming a bubble in the jelly so tight over his face.

Opened, then closed. And then I heard a single word: "Danielle!"

I took a step toward him. But my legs were trembling so hard, I nearly fell.

"Danielle . . ." he repeated, the name bubbling in front of his mouth. "Come, Danielle." He stretched his gray hand to me.

I froze. "Huh?" His hand grazed mine, sticky and wet, and so cold, cold as death.

"Come," he said, the word muffled behind the bubbling slime.

"N-no—!" I gasped. I pulled back.

"They've forgotten you too," he said. As he reached for me, the thick gelatin over his arm stretched with him. "Danielle, you are a Forgotten One now. You must come with us. Come."

Peter took a slow, heavy step away from the open trapdoor. And behind him I saw another figure. A girl, pale as my brother, covered in the wet, sticky goo. She climbed up silently from the pit, her lifeless eyes locked on me.

Behind her another gray kid. And then another.

The forgotten kids.

They climbed out one by one, moving in slow motion, stepping out of the dark pit and circling me.

I tried to break away. But they locked hands and formed a tight ring around me.

"*Come with us. . . .*" they moaned. And the moan became an ugly chant. "*Come with us. . . . Come with us. . . . Come with us. . . .*"

"You are forgotten too," Peter said. "You are one of us."

"*Come with us! Come with us! Come with us!*"

Peter grabbed me with his cold, sticky hands. "Come with us, Danielle."

The circle of kids tightened around me.

Peter pulled me, pulled me hard toward the black pit. I could feel a chill of cold air from below. The sour odor of decay floated up to me.

My stomach lurched.

Peter pulled me closer. Down, down, down to the foul blackness . . .

"*Come with us. . . . Come with us. . . . Come with us. . . .*"

And as the darkness closed around me, I opened my mouth in a scream of horror. "NOOOOOOOOOOOO!"

Still screaming, I broke loose.

With a hard, desperate tug, I tore myself from my brother's sickening grasp. I lowered my shoulders, and with another cry, with scream after scream bursting from my lungs—I tore through the ring of chanting kids.

And hurtled toward the stairs. The foul smell floated with me, heavy and rank. The cold mucus stuck to my hands. My brother's words repeated in my whirring mind: *"They've forgotten you too. . . . They've forgotten you too. . . ."*

No, I'm not! I told myself as I forced my trembling legs up the stairs. I'm not forgotten! I'm not!

"I'll *make* Mom remember!" I shouted down. "Somehow, I'll make Mom remember, Peter!"

I reached the top of the stairs, my chest heaving, my lungs aching.

I slammed the basement door shut and started down the back hall.

The floor spun beneath me. The walls appeared to close in until I felt as if I were running through a dark, narrow tunnel.

What can I do? I asked myself. The whole house seems to be closing in on me. As if I don't belong here anymore.

How can I prove that I'm telling the truth? How can I make Mom remember us?

As I reached the front stairs, a figure jumped out to block my way.

"Dad!" I screamed. "You're home! Please—tell Mom—!"

"Who are you?" he demanded angrily. "You'd better get out of this house. The police are on their way."

"No, Dad—listen!" I pleaded.

"Get out—now!" he shouted.

"No! I live here!" I screamed. "It's my house too! You have to remember us! You have to!"

He dove for me. Tried to capture me.

I dodged to the side. Fell onto the steps. Landing hard on my knees and elbows. Pain shot through my whole body. But I ignored it. Ignored it and scrambled up the stairs on all fours.

At the top, I climbed to my feet. And stared down the long hall.

What can I do? How can I make them remember?

My room! I decided. I'll show them my room. Maybe that will remind them who I am. Maybe that will force them to remember.

I took a few steps—and then stopped.

I stared at the doors on both sides of the hall. Which room is mine? Which one?

"Oh nooooo," I moaned.

My room. I didn't remember my room.

I'm forgetting too. I'm forgetting everything.

Sick with horror, I sank against the wall.

"I'm lost," I murmured. "I give up. I'm lost."

Then something down the hall caught my eye.

I stared at it. Stared at it, forcing myself to remember what it was.

And suddenly, I had an idea.

A rectangle of yellow light fell over the framed photograph on the wall. The photograph of Peter's teddy bear wearing the eyeglasses gleamed as if in a spotlight.

"Yes!" I cried, staring hard at it.

I knew it had something to do with Peter. I didn't remember exactly what. But I knew it was important to my parents.

I tore down the hall, reached up with both hands, and started to pull the photo off the wall.

"What are you doing?" a voice screamed angrily. "Put that down!"

"Get out of this house!"

Mom and Dad came bursting down the hall, their faces red with fury.

"She's up here, Officer!" Dad shouted downstairs. "We have her trapped in the hall!"

The framed photo stuck against its wire. I struggled to pull it free.

"What are you stealing, young woman?" Mom demanded. "Let go of that!"

"Are you crazy? Coming in here like this?" Dad cried.

He grabbed my arm. "Get away from there, miss. The police are here."

A blue-uniformed police officer, tall and blond, hands tensed at his sides, moved into the hallway.

"Here she is," Mom called to him, pointing to me. "She's crazy! Crazy! She just broke in and—and—"

The officer moved toward me menacingly. "Young lady, you'd better come with me," he said softly, blue eyes narrowed on me coldly.

He reached out to grab me.

I tugged the photograph free. My hands were shaking so hard, I nearly dropped it.

I spun around. And raised the photo high.

I held it up to my parents. And I screamed: "NOW TEDDY CAN SEE HOW CUTE I AM!"

I watched Mom and Dad freeze. They stood like open-mouthed statues.

Will they remember? I asked myself. I gripped the frame tightly, held it up as if holding on to life . . . holding on to everything I knew.

Will they remember?

No.

They don't remember.

They're just standing there. Staring at it. Staring at me as if I'm crazy.

No . . . no . . .

And then I saw a single tear run down Dad's cheek.

Mom uttered a cry. And I saw her eyes glisten with tears. "Peter . . . " she whispered.

"Peter . . . " Dad echoed. He stared hard at me. "Danielle!"

He remembered!

n, Danielle," he cried. His voice broke. "I'm so
rry."

And then the three of us were wrapped in a tearful hug.

"You remember!" I cried, still gripping the photograph tightly. "You remember us!"

"Danielle, please—forgive us!" Mom said, pressing her tear-stained cheek against mine.

The police officer shook his head. "What's going on here?" he demanded. "Do you know this girl?"

"Yes," Dad told him. "She's our daughter. We—we can't explain, Officer. We won't be needing you now."

"She—she didn't break in?"

"No," Dad told him. "You can go. Sorry for the trouble. We made a terrible mistake."

The policeman headed away, grumbling to himself, muttering and shaking his head.

"Peter," I choked out. "We have to hurry. We have to get Peter."

I led them down to the basement. "He-he's in the little back room," I told them.

But no.

The room stood empty. Bare, concrete floor. Stone walls. No trapdoor. No opening that led to an endless, black pit.

We're too late, I realized. He's gone.

Mom and Dad stared at me, bewildered. "Where is he?" Mom whispered. "You said—"

"Gone," I murmured. "Lost."

I couldn't stand it. I felt about to explode.

I realized I still had the teddy bear photo. I raised it high, as high as I could reach. "Peter, we remember you!" I screamed. "We remember you! We remember you!"

Silence.

The longest silence of my life.

And then the floor shook, and I heard a low, rumbling sound.

The rumble became a loud groan. The floor raised up . . . up. . . . The trapdoor slowly, heavily creaked open.

We all gasped as Peter stepped forward.

"We remember you!" I cried. "We remember!"

The thick mucus covering dropped from his body, fell off in chunks, rained to the floor, and then melted.

Peter stepped forward, blinking, testing his arms, his legs, stretching.

And then we were hugging. Celebrating. Celebrating the greatest family reunion of all time!

Later I was in Peter's room, helping him unpack some cartons and put the stuff away. It felt good to be doing something useful, something normal.

I kept glancing at the photo of the teddy bear with its eyeglasses. We had set it up on top of the dresser. The bear smiled down at us, as if it too was happy about being remembered.

"Tell me again about how you hypnotized me," Peter said, stacking comic books on a shelf.

"I *didn't* hypnotize you," I answered. "I only thought I did. I thought everything was my fault. But it was never me. It was the evil in this house. But we defeated this house. Thank goodness we defeated it!"

Peter thought about it a while. "I just don't understand how—" he started.

But Mom interrupted, calling from downstairs. "Addie is here!"

I pushed a carton away and hurried down to meet her. "Hi! I'm so glad to see you!" I cried.

She laughed. "Well . . . I'm glad too!"

I led her into the living room. "Everything is back to normal," I told her. "My brother is perfectly fine. And I'm okay. And everything is great! I'm just so *happy*!"

Addie let out a relieved sigh. "I'm so glad to hear it, Brittany. I was so worried about you."

I stared at her. "Excuse me? What did you call me?"

She stared back at me. "Brittany, of course."

My brother poked his head into the room. "Hi, Addie. What's up?"

She grinned at him. "What's up with you, Craig?"

I gasped and grabbed Addie by the shoulder. "What did you call him? Craig? You called us Brittany and Craig?"

Addie frowned. "Of course. What's your problem, Brittany? I should know your names, shouldn't I? I've known you two ever since you moved here with your aunt and uncle."

My mouth dropped open. I gaped at her in horror.

Addie laughed. "Come on. You didn't *really* forget your own names! You're joking, right? *Right*?"

ABOUT THE AUTHOR

R.L. STINE says he has a great job. "My job is to give kids the CREEPS!" With his scary books, R.L. has terrified kids all over the world. He has sold over 300 million books, making him the best-selling children's author in history.

These days, R.L. is dishing out new frights in his series THE NIGHTMARE ROOM. When he isn't working, he likes to read old mysteries, watch *SpongeBob Squarepants* on TV, and take his dog, Nadine, for long walks around New York City, where he lives with his wife, Jane, and son, Matthew.

"I love taking my readers to scary places," R.L. says. "Do you know the scariest place of all? It's your MIND!"

Take a look at what's ahead in
THE NIGHTMARE ROOM #2
Locker 13

I changed into my street clothes. I made my way upstairs to stop at my locker. *Locker 13.*

Basketball practice had run so late, the halls were empty. My shoes clonked noisily on the hard floor. Most of the lights had already been turned off.

This school is creepy when it's empty, I decided. I stopped in front of my locker, feeling a chill at the back of my neck.

I always felt a little weirded-out in front of the locker. For one thing, it wasn't with the other seventh-grade lockers. It was down at the end of the back hall, by itself, just past a janitor's supply closet.

Up and down the hall, all the other lockers had been painted over the summer. They were all a smooth, silvery gray. But no one had touched locker 13. The old, green paint was peeling and had large patches scraped off. Deep scratches criss-crossed up and down the door.

The locker smelled damp. And sour. As if it had once been filled with rotting leaves or dead fish or something.

That's okay, I can deal with this, I told myself.

I took a deep breath. New attitude, Luke. New attitude. Your luck is going to change.

I opened my backpack and pulled out a fat black marker. Then I closed the locker door. And right above the number 13, I wrote the word LUCKY in big, bold capital letters.

I stepped back to admire my work: LUCKY 13.

"Yessss!" I felt better already.

I shoved the black marker into my backpack and started to zip it up. And that's when I heard the breathing.

Soft, soft breaths. So soft, I thought I imagined them. From inside the locker?

I crept closer and pressed my ear against the locker door.

I heard a soft hiss. Then more breathing.

The backpack slipped out of my hands and thudded to the floor. I froze.

And heard another soft hiss inside the locker. It ended in a short cry.

The back of my neck prickled. My breath caught in my throat.

Without realizing it, my hand had gripped the locker handle.

Should I open the door? Should I?

My hand tightened on the handle. I forced myself to start breathing again.

I'm imagining this, I told myself.

There can't be anyone breathing inside my locker.

I lifted the handle. Pulled open the door.

"Hey—!" I cried out in shock. And stared down at a black cat.

The cat gazed up at me, its eyes red in the dim hall light. The black fur stood up on its back. It pulled back its lips and hissed again.

A black cat?

A black cat inside my locker?

I'm imagining this, I thought. I blinked hard, trying to blink the cat away.

A black cat inside locker 13? Could there be any *worse* luck?

"How—how did you get in there?" I choked out.

The cat hissed again and arched its back. It gazed up at me coldly.

Then it leapt from the locker floor. It darted over my shoes, down the hall. Running rapidly, silently. Head down, tail straight up, it turned the first corner, and disappeared.

I stared after it, my heart pounding. I could still feel its furry body brushing against my leg. I realized I was still gripping the locker handle.

My head spun with questions. How long had the cat been in there? How did it get inside the locked door? Why was there a black cat in my locker? Why?

I turned and checked out the floor of the locker. Just to make sure there weren't any other creatures hiding in there. Then, still feeling confused, I closed the door carefully, locked it, and stepped back.

LUCKY 13.

The black letters appeared to glow.

"Yeah. Lucky," I muttered, picking up my backpack. "Real lucky. A black cat in my locker."

I held my lucky rabbit's foot and squeezed it tightly all the way home.

Things are going to change, I told myself. Things have *got* to change. . . .

But in the next few weeks, my luck didn't change at all.

One day after school, I was on my way to the computer lab when I ran into Hannah. "Where are you going?" she asked. "Want to come watch my basketball game?"

"I can't," I replied. "I promised to install some new modems for Mrs. Coffey, the computer teacher."

"Mister Computer Geek strikes again!" she said. She started jogging toward the gym.

I made my way into the computer lab and waved to Mrs. Coffey. She was hunched over her desk, sorting through a tall stack of disks. "Hey, how's it going?" she called.

The computer lab is my second home. Ever since Mrs. Coffey learned that I can repair computers, and upgrade them, and install things in them, I've been her favorite student.

And I have to admit, I really like her too. Whenever I don't have basketball practice, I check in at the computer lab to talk with her and see what needs to be fixed.

"Luke, how is your animation project coming along?" she asked, setting down the disks. She brushed back her blond hair. She has the nicest smile. Everyone likes her because she always seems to enjoy her classes so much.

"I'm almost ready to show it to you," I said. I sat down in front of a computer and started to remove the back. "I think it's really cool. And it's going much faster now. I found a new way to move pixels around."

Her eyes grew wide. "Really?"

"It's a very cool invention," I said, carefully sliding the insides from the computer. "The program is pretty simple. I think a lot of animators might like it."

"Luke . . . I have some big news," she said suddenly. I turned and caught the excited smile on her face. "You're the first person to hear it. Can you keep a secret?"

"Yeah. Okay," I said.

"I just got the most wonderful job! At a really big software company in Chicago. I'm leaving school next week!"

The next afternoon, I couldn't check in at the computer lab. I had to hurry to the swimming pool behind the gym.

Swimming is my other big sport. I spent all last summer working with an instructor at our local pool. He was fast enough to make the Olympic try-outs a few years ago. And he really improved my stroke and showed me a lot of secrets for getting my speed up.

So I looked forward to the try-outs for the Squires swim team. I couldn't wear my lucky swimsuit because it didn't fit anymore. But I wore my lucky shirt to school that day. And as I changed for the pool, I silently counted to seven three times.

As I left the locker room, I heard shouts and laughter echoing off the tile pool walls. Feeling my heart start to race, I stepped into the steamy air of the indoor pool. The floor was puddled with warm water. I inhaled the sharp chlorine smell. I love that smell!

Then I bent down and kissed the top of the diving board. I know. It sounds weird. But it's just something I always do.

I turned to the pool. Three or four guys were already in the water. At the shallow end, I saw Stretch. He was violently splashing two other guys. He had them cornered at the end of the pool. His big hands slapped the water, sending up tall waves over them. They pleaded with him to give them a break.

Coach Swanson blew his whistle, then shouted for Stretch to cut the horseplay. Stretch gave the two guys one more vicious splash.

Then he turned and saw me. "Hey, Champ—" he shouted, his voice booming off the tiles. "You're early. Drowning lessons are *next* week! Ha ha! Nice swim trunks. Are those your *girlfriend's*? Ha ha!"

A few other guys laughed too.

I decided to ignore them. I was feeling pretty confident. About twenty guys were trying out. I knew there were only six spots open on the team. But after all my work last summer, I thought I could make the top six.

Coach Swanson made us all climb out and line up at the deep end of the pool.

"Okay, guys, I've got to get to my night job by five, so we're going to keep this simple," the coach announced. "You have one chance. One chance only. You hear the whistle, you do a speed dive into the pool. You do two complete laps, any stroke you want. I'll take the first six guys. And two alternates. Any questions?"

There weren't any.

Everyone leaned forward, preparing to dive. Stretch lined up next to me. He elbowed me hard in the side. "Give me some room, Champ. Don't crowd me."

The whistle blew. All down the row, bodies tensed, then plunged forward.

I started my dive—and slipped.

The pool floor—so wet . . .

My feet slid on the tile.

Oh . . . no!

I hit the water with a loud *smack*.

A belly flop! No kind of dive. I raised my head, struggling to recover, And saw everyone way ahead of me.

One unlucky slip . . .

I lowered my head, determined to catch up. I started stroking easily, forcing myself to be calm. I remembered the slow, steady, straight-legged kick my instructor had taught me.

I sped up. I passed some guys. Hit the wall and started back.

I can do this, I told myself. I can still make the team.

Faster . . .

At the end of the second lap, the finish was a furious blur. Blue water. Thrashing arms. Loud breaths. Bobbing heads.

I tried to shut out everything and concentrate on my stroke . . . ignore everyone else. . . and SWIM!

At last, my hand hit the pool wall. I ducked under, then surfaced, blowing out water. I wiped my hair away from my eyes. The taste of chlorine was in my mouth. Water running down my face, I glanced around.

I didn't finish last. Some guys were still swimming. I squinted down the line of swimmers who had finished. How many? How many were ahead of me?

"Luke—you're seventh," Coach Swanson

announced. He made a large check on his clipboard. "First alternate. See you at practice."

I was still too out-of-breath to reply.

Seventh.

I let out a long sigh. I felt so disappointed. I could do better than seventh, I knew. If only I hadn't slipped.

I trudged back to the locker room and got dressed quickly, standing in a corner by myself. A few guys came over to say congratulations. But I didn't feel I deserved it.

I tossed my towel in the basket. Then I stepped up to the mirror over the sinks to comb my hair. A ceiling lightbulb was out, and I had to lean over the sink to see.

I had just started to comb my wet hair back— when I saw the jagged crack along the length of the glass.

"Whoa." I stopped combing and stepped back.

A broken mirror. Seven years bad luck for someone.

I reached into my khakis pocket and squeezed my rabbit's foot three times. Then I turned back to the mirror and began combing my hair again.

Something was wrong.

I blinked. Once. Twice.

A red light? Some kind of red glare in the mirror glass.

I squinted into the glass—and let out a cry.

The red glare was coming from a pair of eyes—two red eyes, glowing like hot coals.

Two angry red eyes, floating in the glass. Floating beside my reflection.

I could see my confused expression as I stared at the frightening red eyes . . . as I watched the eyes slide across the glass . . . slide . . . slide closer . . . until their red glow covered MY eyes!

My horrified reflection stared out at me with the fiery, glowing eyes.

And I opened my mouth and let out a long, terrified scream.

JOIN R.L. STINE AND ALL YOUR FRIENDS IN

the NIGHTMARE rOOm

STEP INSIDE
WWW.THENIGHTMAREROOM.COM
AND OPEN THE DOOR TO TERROR!

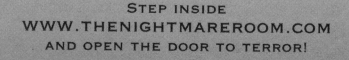

Who will be next to enter

the NIGHTMARE room?